OTHER BOOKS BY
ROBERT VANDERZEE

Encounter with History

Burt Russell Shurly: A Man of Conviction;
A Life in Medicine and Education

The Visitor's Report

The Death of Lois Janeway

TWO BRIDGES TO SIN

A PAUL STEIGER MYSTERY

ROBERT VANDERZEE

TWO BRIDGES TO SIN
A PAUL STEIGER MYSTERY

iUniverse books may be ordered through booksellers or by contacting:

iUniverse
1663 Liberty Drive
Bloomington, IN 47403
www.iuniverse.com
844-349-9409

ISBN: 978-1-6632-0997-9 (sc)
ISBN: 978-1-6632-0998-6 (e)

Library of Congress Control Number: 2020918705

Print information available on the last page.

iUniverse rev. date: 09/28/2020

To my cousin, Dana "Bunny" Wormer Riley, who suggested the title and urged me to write this book. We both grew up on Grosse Ile, Michigan, an island seemingly separated from the real world by its two bridges.

CONTENTS

AUTHOR'S NOTE

I have to tell you about Moorey's Grove. It's a restaurant that appears in several places in the story. There was such a place in the location noted in chapter 2, and except for my fictionalized story of its history, of which I have no actual knowledge, my description of it fits what I remember from my many visits.

Grosse Ile is where I grew up, and Moorey's is where I spent many a Friday or Saturday evening hosting drinks with friends. I have fond memories of the place and miss it being there when I visit now. It was as important a part of my life while I lived in Michigan and later in Akron, Ohio, as it is of Paul Steiger's.

The real Moorey's was owned and operated by a gentleman by the name of Frank Palumbo. He ran the bar, and his wife, Mary, was in charge of the kitchen, where the finest food in the downriver area south of Detroit was prepared. The Palumbos ran a first-class operation for as long as it was open. As I mentioned in the story, when a visitor bellied up to the bar, he was as apt to sit next to a millionaire as he was a working stiff.

Moorey's Grove has been closed since 1988, and nothing replaced it. As of my last visit to the area, the lot where it stood was empty, just a grass lawn surrounded tastefully by boulders, so it won't be disturbed, I suppose. But all the Grosse Ile old-timers remember Moorey's fondly.

CHAPTER 1

AKRON, OHIO

It was Tuesday afternoon when Betty Diamond, a petite blonde with a "don't touch" attitude, stepped into my office. Uptight blondes scare me.

"A Sarabella Norbeck is on your line," she said. "Said to say, 'Don is dead.'"

I jerked up in my chair like I'd been stuck with a cattle prod. "What did you say?"

"I said she said, 'Don is dead.'"

I had lost friends in Iraq, but this was different. Don Norbeck had been my best friend since I was four. I quickly put the phone to my ear.

"Happened four days ago," Sarabella said. "Last Friday. They're calling it suicide. They're full of shit." Sarabella Norbeck was a very delicate society matron, filthy rich, and never wrong—or so she had always said. "The funeral's tomorrow at two. Tomorrow night after the funeral, there will be a dinner at my home for special guests. I want you to attend."

Before I could find words to reply, she spoke again.

"Paul, it wasn't a suicide. You know Don as well as I do."

"He was always up, Mrs. Norbeck." I had to be careful what I said. That was $300 million on the other end of my line.

"Never depressed. He couldn't have done this to himself."

"I agree. He wouldn't do this."

"Not only is it not suicide," she said adamantly, "but I know who did this to him."

"You know?"

"I have it narrowed down, and I'm inviting them to the dinner. You'll meet them."

"Isn't this something for the police?"

"Paul, the police could be involved. Why else would they come to such a conclusion with no evidence?"

I didn't answer.

"You're coming to dinner here, and I'm going to announce that you're in charge of my investigation—death threats or no death threats."

"*Death* threats?"

"Yes … yes. They want to kill me too."

"Well, Mrs. Norbeck, I'll come to your dinner, and I want to be at the funeral. But we're going to have to talk about any kind of investigation. I really think you need trained professionals for this."

"Nonsense. Don told me about your Janeway adventure a couple of years ago. You know how to handle yourself."

She was referring to a criminal conspiracy to take over the company I had worked for in Akron three years ago, an affair that nearly cost me my life—twice.

"This won't be anything like that. You'll meet the suspects at dinner. For you, the investigation will be duck soup."

"I'll be there, but we'll have to talk. A long talk after dinner."

"Yes, by all means. Then you'll be a guest in my home until you find the killer."

"We have to talk."

"Paul, you just be here for the funeral," she said and hung up.

I returned the phone to its cradle and leaned back in my chair to retrieve memories of Sarabella Norbeck's family on that long, slim island south of Detroit that cut the Detroit River in two as it emptied its water into Lake Erie. It was an island of ten thousand souls connected to the real world by two narrow bridges. French explorers named it Grosse Ile in 1679.

I hurriedly arranged to take some of the vacation I'd accumulated. Three hours after Sarabella's call, my Akron condo in the Moeller Building was locked and I was in my aged BMW heading west on the Ohio Turnpike with empty lungs and a slow burn in my gut. I had one small suitcase in the trunk and a sport jacket folded on the back seat. I planned to stay several days this time. Losing Don would require more than just a quick hello/goodbye to friends and relatives.

I had lots of time to think about the Norbeck family during the journey. Don and I were two years old when his father died, so we never knew him. But I heard his older brother, Bertie, was a lot like him—well educated, lazy, mild mannered, and kept to himself. When we were growing up, Don and I had little to do with Bertie. We thought he was a fink, and to him we were pests.

But Don's sister, Susan, was something else. I still had the scars to show for my time with her. She had the looks and personality of her mother. By the time I was in tenth grade, I was hopelessly in love with her—my first love. And she knew it. She dropped me for a football hero who was in his junior year, then wanted me back when the guy graduated. I don't mind admitting I was hurt real deep.

I still had a crush on her but knew that I would never renew the relationship. Beautiful, spoiled, cunning, vile tempered, Susan was addicted to sex and alcohol—a real mess. I blamed Sarabella.

CHAPTER 2

MOOREY'S GROVE

Traffic in Toledo was heavy that afternoon, so it was after nine thirty when I rolled into the Moorey's Grove parking lot. A decided chill hung in the air as I stepped out of the car.

Moorey's was a small, low-key bar-restaurant located about a mile south of the road leading to a bridge over the Detroit River to the island of Grosse Ile. I could find it blindfolded. Hell, I could find it blind drunk, and that had occurred more times than I cared to remember.

I always stopped at Moorey's whenever I returned to Grosse Ile, pretty much out of habit. Every time, I would enter the building and salute Jake Kubiak at work behind the bar, my signal for him to start my first gin martini of the evening. Then I would glance around for friends, rich and poor, some of whom were sure to be there.

Jake was the owner and chief bartender, and he liked it that way, and so did I. So did a lot of people. Jake served industrial-grade martinis, good food, and real conversation. What else mattered?

This evening was no different from any other. I parked my car in the nearly full parking lot, walked through the door, and turned right. A row of eight dimly lit, comfortably upholstered, six-person booths were arranged along the wall to my right. I was greeted by the usual murmur of voices, the usual music from somewhere, and the usual stale atmosphere bars get from six beer spigots working overtime. Jake was there looking at me.

"Paul! Where you been? I ain't seen you in a while."

"You remember me after three years?"

"Absolutely. You helped pay for the place. Where you been? Sit your ass down. I'll get a martini going for you."

"I been out of the country," I said as I eased my six-foot-two frame onto one of only two empty barstools. "Over in Europe."

"So I hear." Jake turned over a glass, filled it with ice and vermouth, stirred it, added Beefeater gin in a three-to-one ratio, dropped in an olive, and handed it to me. He gave a serious look. "You hear about Don?"

"That's why I'm here. The funeral's tomorrow." I sipped the martini. The passing of three years hadn't caused him to lose his touch.

"I can't believe he did it. That wasn't the Don Norbeck I knew."

"I understand there are some questions," I said, "but I guess the cops are saying he did it, and the coroner agrees." I swirled the ice around the glass with my finger. I always thought my finger added a special touch.

Jake looked away and didn't answer immediately. He looked like he was trying to frame a comment about the Grosse Ile police that wouldn't offend a guy who had grown up there. "Maybe they know something."

I nodded but didn't say anything—just looked down.

Visit Moorey's any hour of the day or night, and you were as likely to sit next to a millionaire as a working stiff. When I first started going there, age nineteen, the decor was, let's say, early thirties Prohibition. The place had started as a speakeasy in the late twenties and had only recently mellowed into late-fifties rock concert in its struggle toward the twenty-first century.

I looked around and spotted a couple of guys I knew and hadn't seen in a long time, their heads together in deep discussion. They were two very different people—close friends, but you wouldn't know it by the way they needled each other: Tom McGraw and Bill Gordon, older than me by maybe twenty years. They'd kind of taken me under their wing when I started showing up at Moorey's underage about ten years ago and taught me how to drink.

They'd been through the Vietnam War and had been deeply affected by their experiences. Tom had volunteered for the army immediately out of college, determined to help turn the Communist tide. By the time his enlistment was up, he'd seen firsthand how McNamara had led LBJ into a no-win, politically directed war of massive American casualties. The experience had destroyed Tom's drive to succeed. He was now working harder not to work than most guys do to find work.

Bill, on the other hand, had never had a drive to succeed. College hadn't been for him. Instead, upon graduating from high school, he asked for and received from his very wealthy parents a large semitruck he would drive to make what little money he would need for his weekends at Moorey's. When the Vietnam War arrived, the government drafted him into the navy. The truck was waiting for him when he returned.

I looked over at those two guys again and saw they had a girl with them. "Jake, I see some friends over there I need to say hello to." I slipped off my stool, picked up what was left of the "tini," and headed to the fourth booth from the door.

The girl with them was a trim honey-blonde, her long hair swept back into a high ponytail. She was attractive, and there was something about her. I wondered if I'd seen her before and who she was and if the evening was going to get complicated. They looked up when I got to their table.

"I knew you'd be here," I said before they could say anything.

"Welcome home, buddy!" Bill said.

"Good to be home."

"How long you been back from Europe?"

"About three weeks."

"For Christ's sake! It took you three weeks to get here?"

"Tonight's my first chance to get away," I said, sitting down beside the girl. "I've got a job in Akron, you know."

The girl inched herself and her drink away from me and toward Bill. She looked at me with intelligent gray eyes. "I'm Joan Worth. I haven't seen you around."

"Paul Steiger."

She continued eyeing me. "Name sounds familiar."

"I'm from Grosse Ile originally. Went to school here."

"Oh, yeah. I remember now. Grosse Ile class of '88."

"How would you know that?"

"Actually, I do know you."

"Really?"

"You wouldn't remember me," she said, looking down at her drink.

"Why's that?"

"I was four years behind you in school. You wouldn't have noticed me."

"Paul," Tom cut in, "finish that drink, and I'll buy you another."

"Go ahead and order," I said. "I'll be ready." I glanced at Joan. "And why isn't this gorgeous lady sitting between you two guys for protection against the gangsters that hang out in this place?"

"Trust me," Bill said. "She can handle herself."

Tom turned to me. "I take it you heard about your buddy Don Norbeck."

I nodded. "Would you believe Sarabella Norbeck herself phoned me this afternoon? Wants me to look into it. Doesn't believe it's a suicide."

"Police say it is." Bill scooped some peanuts out of the little porcelain cup on the table and popped one into his mouth. "After Chuck LaGrange found the body, the coroner did a quickie postmortem. Carbon monoxide poisoning written all over Don's face—bright red, they say."

I snagged the remaining nuts before Bill could finish them off. "Yeah, well, Sarabella thinks they're full of shit." I turned to Joan. "Sorry for the language. That's the way she put it."

She broke into an easy smile. "I think I've heard the word before."

I grinned, holding her gaze for a split second, then turned my attention back to the guys. "Sarabella's throwing out all kinds of accusations. What're you guys hearing?"

"We were just talking about it before you got here," Joan said. "One story goes that his wife did it. You did know he got married while you were away?"

"I'd heard."

"Everybody's saying the day he died, they had a big fight and she took off for New York, where she's from. You know his temper. She got to the airport and changed her mind. Turned around. Headed back. But before she got home, she decided it might be a good idea to get one of the cops on Grosse Ile to follow her home, seeing as how Don might still be violent. She and Sergeant LaGrange entered the house. She checked upstairs. He checked the kitchen and garage. Don was on the garage floor, dead, car engine running. Looks like suicide to the cops. Heard there wasn't even an autopsy."

"Why the doubts?"

"Don had a knot on his head. Maybe she popped him a good one while he was working on the car, then closed the garage door and walked away."

"Anyone could've done that," Tom said. "Didn't have to be her."

"You're right. Anyone could've. Hell, you could've." Bill turned to Joan. "You had the hots for Don once upon a time before he left for New York. Maybe *you* did it in a fit of jealousy."

"Goddamn it, you know I got over him a long time ago."

"So you say."

"I couldn't give a crap when he returned home married. Besides, how could I object? She's a nice person. You guys remember the night we met her. We were right here, sitting in the next booth over." She looked over at the booth in question. "Anyway, they came in and sat down with us, had a few, and we got to know her. I came away liking her."

"We all liked her," Tom said.

"She's definitely New York society," Joan said, "but doesn't act it. She's way out of our league, but you can't help liking her."

"And people think she did it?"

"There isn't a chance in hell she did it," Joan said. "If you want to look into it, go ahead, but it wasn't her."

"I wouldn't even know where to start."

"We'll help any way we can. Right, guys?"

They nodded.

I took a breath. "Well, Mrs. Norbeck wants me to look into it. I suppose I'm going to have to visit LaGrange after the funeral and find out what he knows ..." At this point, I lost my train of thought. I pointed my thumb at a tough-looking dude sitting on one of the barstools. He'd been looking at us for most of the time I'd been there. He was dressed in a black T-shirt and black pants. He was mostly looking at me—boring holes in me—and it was beginning to bother me. "Who's that?" I asked.

"That's Eric Gitano," Tom said. "An asshole, if you have to know. He's with Societe Inter Nationale."

CHAPTER 3

SOCIETE INTER NATIONALE

My eyes shifted to each of them in succession. "What the hell's Societe Inter Nationale?"

They looked away, each fingering the drinks in front of them.

Finally, Tom looked at me. "They bought the old Norbeck mansion."

"So what's the big deal?"

"Well, it seems they've turned it into a Playboy Club—on steroids."

"So who's he?"

"He's their chief muscle."

"Why's he staring at me?"

"Maybe because you're new in town. Hasn't seen you around. Just checking you out."

"Maybe I should go over and introduce myself."

"Not a good idea," Tom said. "Don't pay any attention to him. He loves to piss people off."

They were silent again for a time.

Finally, Joan turned to me, her expression serious. "A lot's happened since you went away."

"Societe Inter Nationale is some European outfit," Bill said. "French, I think. They run gentlemen's clubs." He air-quoted the phrase. "You know—cocktails, dining, gaming tables. A whole lot of drugs and twisted sex. Way beyond anything Hefner ever conceived of. You've never seen anything like it."

I raised an eyebrow. "And you have?"

"Don't be cute. It's what people have been saying."

"What do they want with that old mansion?"

Bill sniffed. "You mean the *renovated* mansion, complete with third-floor party room and living quarters. They even carved up the top floors so you can stand up there and see clear down to the first. Now it's closed for more work."

"Don't forget their glass elevator built for two in a horizontal position." Tom took a swig of his beer. "They call it sky-fuck."

"Old Sam would shit if he saw what they were doing to his mansion," Bill said.

"Oh, I don't know," Tom said. "I heard he was a party boy. Sam was a heavy drinker, told lots of stories, and was the life of the party until he had one too many. When he got that way, Don said he could switch from fun guy to obnoxious asshole in midsentence. Maybe that's why he was murdered."

"Yeah but very straitlaced when it came to sex."

Tom tapped the back of my hand. "'Member them two slips Sam Norbeck had for his experimental boats? He used to back those babies in, just in case he needed to make a quick getaway."

"He was paranoid," Bill said.

"It ain't paranoia if people actually hate you." Tom shot his friend a look. "Anyway, they expanded them to hold two big yachts."

"And here's the kicker," Bill said. "They left the old gate intact, including the old man's initials."

I pictured the ugly, wrought iron monstrosity my pals and I used to climb during our many clandestine visits to the property in search of the elusive Sam Norbeck safe room. "Why in God's name would they do that?"

"It makes a certain kind of sense," he explained. "Societe Inter Nationale. Samuel Irwin Norbeck." A sly smile crept onto Bill's face.

Half a beat later, I rolled my eyes as my brain made the connection. "You've got to be shittin' me."

"I shit you not, my friend. We call it the *Sin* Club." Satisfied with himself, Bill leaned back against the booth. "Pretty goddamned big deal for lil' old conservative Grosse Ile."

"How'd they ever get approval to operate on Grosse Ile?" I asked.

"We never allowed a liquor license on the island. Never, as long as I can remember."

"Money," Joan said.

"You remember how long the Norbecks had been trying to unload the place," Tom added. "Years. When Sarabella got a nibble from Societe Inter Nationale, she and their head guy went to the local movers and shakers and made them an offer they couldn't believe."

"How much?"

"Don't know, but it had to be huge money."

"Come on. How much?"

"I don't know. But wait until you see what Societe Inter Nationale did for our little island. New roads and new schools. The airport is modern now—lengthened one of the runways for their jet. The whole island shines. They bought the police with a brand-new police station. State-of-the-art. I'm telling you, you won't believe it."

"And now the township has reduced our property taxes," Bill added. "So no one's complaining. Remember how it was so high because there was no industry on the island?"

"I can tell you some people around here are sporting new second and third homes around the world," Joan said. "Money can bring happiness to a lot of people."

"How do you know all that?" I asked.

"In my business, word gets around. I work for a publishing house in Detroit."

"Lucky you."

"Don had wanted us to edit and publish his book when he got it done."

"Book?" Now I was even more puzzled.

"Oh, I guess you don't know about Don's book," Joan said. "Don was writing a book about the Norbeck family. You probably know some of that Norbeck history."

"I lived two doors away from them growing up. I heard a lot of stories."

"Don wanted to write it all down," Joan said. "He was looking around for someone to publish it."

"Tell me about it."

"The book was going to be about old Sam and the inventions that made him all his money. It told about Sam's marriage to Marion and what kind of guy he was according to people around town and relatives who'd known him. It describes Sam's mansion and details of his escape tunnel."

"When are you going to publish it?"

"We aren't. We turned him down."

I put my drink down and looked at her. "Why?"

"Death threats."

"You got death threats too?"

"My boss did."

"From who?"

"Pretty sure they came from Gitano, the guy over there staring daggers at you. That's why we dropped it. We're not heroes."

"Sarabella says she's getting death threats," I said.

"The rumors say Don continued with the book," Joan said. "Added spicy details about Societe Inter Nationale and the Norbeck family."

"So where's the manuscript now?" I asked.

"Gave it back to Don."

"Would Don have given a copy to Societe Inter Nationale?"

Joan sat back in the booth and looked at me like it was a dumb question. "No human way. He wouldn't tell them anything."

"So how come our friend Gitano knows about it?"

Joan shrugged. "I don't know, but it would explain the death threats. We think Don was finding out some bad stuff about Societe Inter Nationale."

Keeping his voice low, Tom said, "There's something real bad going on there, and the only way to find out is to become a member of the club and join in the fun. And then once you're a member, you find excellent reasons not to say anything. We hear that if you forget, Gitano reminds you."

"If they suspected Don was writing a book about them," Joan said, "they could easily be spreading death threats."

I thought for a minute, then looked at Joan. "Maybe your boss went back to them for a statement. That's what publishers do, don't they?"

"Yeah, but in this case, the death threats came before my boss could contact them."

Our conversation drifted to other subjects, and before anyone could suggest another round, I looked at my watch. I stood up. "It's time for me to go."

"See you tomorrow," Joan said with a smile.

"That would be terrific. Where?"

"At the funeral. You're going to be there, aren't you?" She looked down, slowly worked herself out of the booth, stood, and smoothed her slacks.

Tom was standing now. "You're staying with me tonight," he told me. "As usual. Follow me home."

"I always do as I'm told."

Joan rolled her eyes. "Why don't I believe that?"

As we headed out the door, I found myself wondering how Eric Gitano could know about Don's manuscript. Of course, the last thing Don would do was advertise any bad stuff he'd found, and if Societe Inter Nationale was throwing around death threats, there was no way Don had committed suicide.

And yes, the evening had gotten complicated. I was looking forward to seeing Joan Worth tomorrow. And for now at least, the gut burn was gone.

CHAPTER 4

THE FUNERAL

It was late morning when I woke up in Tom's condo, pulled myself together, put on clean skivvies, and appeared in the kitchen for breakfast. It was no surprise that he wasn't up yet, so I helped myself to some orange juice and started the coffee. I was into my second piece of toast when he finally trudged in and sat down.

"Coffee, please," he muttered. Tom looked better than he had a right to, given the length of last night's workout.

"You're in luck," I said. "Still two cups left. Thanks again for the sack."

We both looked at opposite walls for some time with nothing to say.

Finally Tom said, "You must have quite a job. Europe for three years, back here for three weeks, and then you just take off. I wish I'd found a boss like yours."

"He's a good guy. Flexible. He understands. But he's not going to take this shit if I'm gone for more than a week. When I got back from London, he put me in an office. I share a young secretary with two others. He already has me starting on another big installation for a tire company overseas."

"You find a place yet?"

"Same place. You remember. You were there once."

"Not bad at all."

We resumed staring at opposite walls. I finished my coffee and headed into my room to dress.

"What time's the funeral?" Tom said. "I'd like to go."

"Two o'clock at Saint James, but why do you want to go? You never liked him all that much."

"I know, but I think I should."

◆

Stepping inside Saint James Episcopal on Grosse Ile's East River Road was like stepping back in time—in more ways than one. The old church, consecrated in 1868 by Bishop Samuel Allen McCroskry, had been mostly funded by a former slave, Lisette Denison Forth, and was listed on the National Register of Historic Places. For many years on Sundays, Don's parents and mine had herded us kids inside its vertical board-and-batten walls to redeem our sins and endure hourlong sermons that seemed to last for days.

I breathed in the long-lingering scent of the building's Carpenter Gothic frame construction as I strode inside the sanctuary and peered at the not-so-big sea of mourners scattered among the pews. At the front sat Sarabella Norbeck herself, flanked by her remaining adult children, Susan and Bertie. I liked Sarabella. She didn't put on airs like so many of the wealthy women on the island did, and her way of speaking, prone to saltiness at times, I had always found to be good for a laugh—out of the range of her hearing, of course.

To this very minute, though, I hadn't a clue about which of her three children she liked or disliked. She could be both loving and vicious within the same breath, often resorting to threats of disinheritance anytime any of them displeased her. In her worst moments, she would proclaim that Don, Bertie, and Susan were God's punishment for her past sins—though, oddly or not, she never ventured to elaborate.

I moved along the east wall, past the eleven-by-six-foot stained glass Tiffany window, *Angel of Praise*, and down the aisle, slipping into the pew two rows back of the family, where Mattie, the Norbecks' housekeeper, sat alone, tears streaming down her ruddy cheeks.

She gripped my arm as I lowered myself onto the cold, hard, dark oak bench. "*Dia Duit*, boy," she crooned in her native Irish. "If you're not a sight for sore eyes."

I had long suspected that the firm yet fiercely caring Mattie O'Toole was the one to sort out and repair much of the psychological damage Sarabella had inflicted on her children over the years, just as I suspected now that it was Mattie O'Toole who was most troubled by Don's passing. I gave her hand a squeeze and forced myself to face the altar, where my best friend lay in a closed casket of brilliant white and gold.

This would be Don's last visit to Saint James.

The funeral was grim and sad as they always are, and unexpectedly short as they usually aren't, and it brought back exuberant and painful memories of Don and me when we began to experience life. The sermon made no mention of how he died, and it ended with an announcement that following the service there would be a reception at the church pavilion next door.

I didn't catch up to the Norbeck family until I entered the reception hall, where they had formed a receiving line. Susan, first in the line, nudged me as I approached, tossing back her long, straight, blond hair.

"Hi there, good-lookin'," she said. "Back from Europe, I see." Her pale blue eyes twinkled in a way seldom seen at a funeral.

"Got here last night. What a hell of a jolt."

"So how've you been? How's your love life? Getting lucky?"

"Afraid not. Still single."

"That's a relief. Still a chance for me, eh?"

"Susan, I really don't think so. We don't need to start that all over again."

By now, she had worked a breast up against my arm.

I edged away from her, but not far enough, and slowly shook my head. "No point in even trying." I couldn't help noticing her perfume. Loud. Expensive.

"Oh, I don't mind trying."

Bertie, next in line, broke away from his place beside his mother and pushed past Susan to shake my hand. "Hi, Paul. Thanks for coming." Bertie had an intelligent look about him. He was a big guy, taller than me, and sported a soft, protruding girth that torso muscles were surrendering to gravity.

"I'm so sorry for your loss."

"It wasn't suicide," he whispered. "These cops are nuts." He noticed

Susan up against me and whispered, "Susan, would you please? This is a church, not a whorehouse."

She glared at him as if to say, "How dare you talk to me like that," but finally did back off.

Out of Susan's hearing, Bertie said, "She's not well. Stay away from her. You're not doing her any good letting her rub up to you like that."

"She's getting worse? Is that possible?"

"I think so. Just stay away from her."

"No problem there. I got over it a long time ago. But, Bertie, you'll have to admit she's absolutely stunning. She's only gotten more beautiful. Those eyes are hypnotic."

Bertie nodded slightly. "Yeah, but I think she's sicker now too. She's run up debts at the Sin Club like you wouldn't believe. Hell, she owes every bar and club in Detroit and downriver. I don't think anyone runs her a tab anymore."

"So how's your mother? I have to say I've never seen her look better. At least from a distance."

"She's still her old self." Bertie smiled. "A rusty pistol that goes off when you least expect it."

"I always liked her," I said. "She could be mean to you kids. But she loves you. I know that. Has she ever stopped threatening to take you out of the will?"

"Not really. Sometimes I think she means it." Bertie's smile was gone.

I frowned. "Bullshit, Bertie. She'd never do that to you and Susan."

"I'm never sure." His eyes narrowed, and he looked around to avoid mine.

Just then, Joan Worth moved into the line next to us and said, "Bertie, I'm so sorry."

"Joan … good to see you here. Glad you could make it. Let me introduce Paul Steiger."

"I know Paul. Met him last night. Hi, Paul."

Joan had arrived in a black dress topped by a conservative gold necklace and matching earrings. Her blond hair was pulled back in the same ponytail as last night.

Susan nudged up against me again, looked at Joan, and said, "Good to see you, Joan, but don't try to steal this guy. He's mine."

"Susan, knock it off," I said. "Joan's an old friend."

Susan gripped my arm, pressing against it again, and looked at me. "Come on. Let's be friends."

"We *are* friends," I said. "And so is Joan. And it's been a long time since I've seen her. She and I have some catching up to do."

Joan nudged me along. "You've never met Don's wife—or I should say widow—have you? That's her, next in line."

"Ellie," Joan said. "This is Paul Steiger. An old friend of Don's."

Mrs. Donald Norbeck extended a hand and looked up, her bright blue eyes conveying a mixture of warmth and sadness. "At last we meet."

"Indeed," I said. "I wish I'd been able to make it to the wedding."

She offered a weak smile while tucking a blade of shoulder-length blond hair behind an ear. "Don explained you were out of town."

"In Europe, yes."

Her eyes wandered beyond my shoulder and came back with a noticeable hint of fear. She brought a nervous hand to the single strand of pearls around her neck—a fitting complement to her tasteful black shift. "Now's not a good time to talk," she said, leaning in. "Could you stop by the house before you return to Akron?"

"Count on it."

As Ellie Norbeck drew back and greeted the next mourner, I noted her perfect oval face and upturned nose and let out a whistle in my mind. Don and I had always had the same taste in women. I turned away from her, already with the feeling that Ellie and I had met somewhere, probably in my dreams.

We moved on to Sarabella. "Mrs. Norbeck, I'm so sorry."

"I am too, Paul. He was a fine son. We had big hopes for him." Then, with a voice I could hardly hear over the noise of the crowd, she said, "Plan on visiting me at home this afternoon."

"I will. When would you like me there?"

"Make it four. We have a lot to discuss."

"I will indeed. Four on the dot."

By now, a substantial line of mourners had formed, pressing us forward.

"Shall we make the rounds?" Joan said.

"By all means."

She ushered me past Sarabella, through the crowd, to a waiter holding a tray of glasses half-filled with white wine. Just ahead, I spotted Dickie Reardon and his wife, Anne.

Anne had large, mournful brown eyes and an underhung jaw that seemed to cause a downward curl to the edges of her mouth. She wore a loose-fitting black dress that couldn't hide a serious weight issue she had given up trying to conquer years ago. When Dickie married her, she had been cute and well proportioned. But soon after the marriage, she'd let herself go. As long as I had known her, there was a melancholy about her that said her world was one of little hope and much despair.

How Dickie had married such a person was a mystery to us all. Dickie was the opposite. No one I knew thought more of his looks and physical appearance than Dickie Reardon. He was tall, body by Gold's Gym, and convinced that the world—and particularly the world's women—adored him. He'd preceded me through the small Grosse Ile school by one year, so I knew him pretty well. Now he was Ellie's next-door neighbor.

"Hi, Dickie," I said. "Long time no see."

Anne nodded to me and forced a smile.

Dickie Reardon said, "Paul, I'm no longer 'Dickie.' No one calls me that anymore. Call me Dick."

"I apologize, Dick. I seem to remember Don always called you Dickie."

"Don't push it, Paul."

Joan tugged at my arm. "Paul, you have more people to meet. Goodbye ... Dick."

We moved off into the crowd.

"You shouldn't antagonize him," she said. "If you're going to look into Don's death, you're going to have to talk to him about it. He was one of Don's partners in a business venture Don was pushing. Don came back from New York to start up an automobile research company. Dick had some money in it, and recently they were not on the best of terms."

"I didn't know that."

"I need to fill you in on a lot of things that have happened in the past three years, but this isn't the place. Right now, you have more people to meet."

"How about that distinguished guy over there? He looks important."

Joan looked away. "Sorry, not him. That's Charles Legro. Manages

Societe Inter Nationale. So phony, so self-important he makes my stomach turn. He's worse than Gitano."

"Who?"

"You know—the guy you saw at Moorey's last night."

"I got a hunch I'm going to have to meet him sooner or later."

Joan smiled. "Make it later. Turn around. Here's Cal Bridges and his wife, Kelli."

I'd never met his wife, but I knew Cal from way back in the days when I had more time to spend at Moorey's. Joan nudged him, and after our hellos, he introduced me to Kelli. We talked of happier days.

"I hear you're here to look into Don's passing," he said after a time. "Find anything yet?"

"Not really. I just got here. Sarabella said something about wanting me to check some things out, but that's all."

"You have some deep shit to wade into."

"I'll only be here a few days. Not likely I'll even get into shallow shit."

"There *is* no shallow shit here, my friend. You're going to find out it's all deep."

I thought that was a curious thing to say. Was he trying to tell me something but not in front of his wife or Joan? Maybe he wanted me to phone him. I wasn't going to, of course. I didn't need deep shit in my life. I'd had my fair share in Iraq. And I had a job in Akron to get back to.

———◆———

"Thanks for getting us out of that church. Maybe you noticed funerals aren't really my thing."

"I suspected a tour in Iraq might have dimmed your interest in them," Joan said. "It was time for lunch, and this place was close. Ever been here?"

"Alice's Lunch didn't exist the last time I was on Grosse Ile."

Alice's Lunch was a small luncheonette on Macomb Street about a mile from the church. A linoleum floor, three neon beer signs at strategic locations on walls about the color of lemon chiffon cake, ten four-place tables, and a small mirror behind a bar with eight stools for single diners pretty well defined the place. The kitchen was out of sight, but I could hear and smell a lot of activity going on back there. The place was only half-full, so we had our pick of the tables.

Joan had gradually worked us toward the door of the church after departing Cal and Kelli, and when I realized what she was thinking, I grabbed her arm and pulled. I'd had enough talking to strangers, and it was lunchtime, and I asked her what was good. Ten minutes after leaving the church, we were here.

I waited until we'd ordered before I began a short recounting of my life. I skimmed over my eight years in the army after college without mentioning the blood or the battle that produced my career-ending PTSD. I said a little more about joining Henderson Engineering, a medium-sized engineering firm in Akron, and I briefly mentioned a Mafia attempt to infiltrate Henderson that involved a mysterious lady. I stopped short of mentioning the emerald smuggling and the contract killings in New Mexico.

Joan listened to every word, hardly touching her sandwich. "So, for you, life hasn't been boring since leaving the army. Any plans to settle down?"

"I was quite settled when Sarabella called yesterday. I'll be quite settled again when I get back to Akron next week. Guaranteed."

"I wonder," Joan said. "You seem to attract trouble like flypaper."

"Just give me a chance. I'll prove it."

"You're on."

I looked at my watch. "Hey, I have to go. Sarabella wants me there at four."

I left a tip, paid the bill, and walked to my car, and she to hers. She looked back and waved before getting in.

CHAPTER 5

SARABELLA BRIEFS ME

As I drove to the Norbeck home, I reminded myself about how she was a crafty old gazillionaire used to getting her own way. *Be very polite, but be firm. Don't let her talk you into anything you don't want to do. You have a job in Akron, Ohio. You have to get back to it. Remember—you are not a detective. Remember ...*

I arrived promptly at four as directed and turned into the winding gravel driveway that led past a hundred feet of mature oaks and maples and an assortment of tall bushes that almost hid her three-story, eight-bedroom home from the street. The driveway curved to the right side of the home past a wide, reddish brick walkway that provided access to a front door guarded by heavy columns supporting an overhang. For all its sculptured woodwork and ornate cast-iron knocker, however, the front door was never used except on formal occasions. It was heavy, and to open it, one had to unlatch the lock and push—hard. I drove on past the kitchen door to the four-car, two-story, detached garage behind the home. I parked and walked to the kitchen door.

This was the home I remembered so well from my childhood. The Norbecks were not big spenders, never flaunted their money, and their home on Grosse Ile reflected these values. Built in 1965, it by no means represented the latest in architecture that the newly married, very young, and very rich Irwin Norbeck could have easily afforded. Instead, Sarabella had selected, with Irwin's approval, a traditional white clapboard colonial to blend with the older nineteenth-century homes arranged along Grosse Ile's traditional Park Lane and East River Road.

Twelve years after Sam Norbeck's death in 1960, Sarabella and Irwin invited his mother, Marion Smith Norbeck, and her housekeeper, Mattie, to stay so the mansion she and Sam had lived in could be put up for sale. The mansion didn't sell and remained empty. Local kids, myself included, broke in from time to time so we could explore its rooms and the hidden passages Sam had installed to evade his enemies, but we never found the safe room he'd been trying to get to when he was murdered.

Marion died in 1975 at age seventy from a stomach ailment, and the Marion Norbeck estate was inherited lock, stock, and barrel by Sarabella and Irwin. Soon after, Irwin committed suicide, leaving everything to Sarabella.

Mattie met me at the door when I walked in, and we hugged. She was a short, strong woman with a permanent look of disapproval etched into her face. Born and raised in Ireland with strong Catholic parents who had died in an armed revolt against the Crown of England, she was in charge of the household and still held the respect of us kids in an iron grip to this day.

I had been to the home so often through the years that Mattie was as much my mother as she had been to Bertie, Don, and Susan. Those had been happy years, but now Mattie's eyes were red, and tears welled up again and were all down her cheeks when I walked in.

Her strong arms surrounded me as she buried her face in my chest. It was a long, long minute before she could find words.

"Paul, good to have you back with us. Don was my favorite, but don't you ever tell the other kids."

"I promise. And as long as we're keeping secrets, you're my favorite mother."

"Now, don't you say that, young man. We both know you love your own mother. Down in Florida somewhere now, is she?"

"They've been there several years now. Dad has the boat he always wanted, and Mom loves the trips they take on it around Florida. Living in Port St. Lucie in a beautiful gated community. Happy as escaped thieves."

"We all miss your family. They're good people. Now go on in and see Mrs. Norbeck. She's waiting for you in the library. I'll lead the way."

We passed through the dining room, down the long, dark hall and past the living room—which was never used—with its portrait of Irwin Norbeck over the large stone fireplace staring in judgment. Memories of

Don were everywhere. When we were kids, Don visited me at home, or I visited him here.

The gut burn was back in spades. I wondered if it would ever end.

I opened the library door for Mattie, nodded thanks, and we stepped inside. Sarabella Norbeck was sitting on the leather couch facing the stone fireplace. Bertie was sitting next to her. She leaned forward with her head turned to see me as I entered. This was the Sarabella Norbeck I remembered from three years ago.

The electricity in her eyes remained, though it had dimmed. "So good of you to come by, Paul," she said quietly, motioning me to a chair across from her. "Mattie, bring Paul a Coke. Too early for martinis, don't you think, Paul?"

"Good to see you, Mrs. Norbeck, even under such bad circumstances. And yes, it is a bit early to start. I would love a Coke."

Mattie left the room and soon returned with my Coke in a glass with ice.

"How are you feeling, Mrs. Norbeck?"

"Not so good. Can't seem to shake this depression. Thank God for Bertie here. He's taking such good care of me."

"Hi, Bertie."

"Good to have you back in town, Paul," Bertie said. "Hope you can stay a few days."

"That's doubtful. I just got back from Europe, and I have a lot to do catching up at work."

Before I could comment further, Sarabella raised her hand for silence and looked to Mattie and Bertie. "I want you two out of the room. I have some business to discuss with Paul."

"Mother, you need me here," Bertie said, eyebrows up.

"I do not. Please leave me with Paul. I'm fine."

"You're not fine, and you know it."

"Damn it, I said get out!"

Mattie had already started to leave, and now Bertie followed her to the door. After the door closed behind them, Mrs. Norbeck turned toward me.

"To begin, Paul, I want you to start calling me Sarabella. You're old enough now. Besides, you're the best of all Don's friends. I wish you'd been one of my sons."

"Thank you, Mrs. ... excuse me, Sarabella. I've always admired you."

Sarabella, still wearing the snug-fitting black dress she'd worn to the funeral, straightened on the couch and adjusted her trademark triple strand of pearls. "Let me start by telling you what I think of this whole goddamned situation."

I stifled a chuckle. "Still a straight shooter, I see."

"Damn right I am." A hint of a smile tugged at her rose-colored lips before her expression grew serious. "First of all, as I told you on the phone, my son did not kill himself. You know as well as I that he wasn't capable of such a thing. He was too full of life and ambition."

"Last I checked, that was the case."

"I mean, can you really see Don sitting in his car, engine running, with garage door down, patiently waiting to die?"

My mind went back to the night before and the conversation at Moorey's. Hadn't Joan said Don was found on the *floor* of the garage?

"Well?"

I jolted back to the present. Sarabella was staring me down with those electric eyes of hers. As a kid, I had been convinced she could see clear through to my thoughts. I never told her a single lie.

"It is hard to imagine," I conceded.

"You better believe it is. He was too active and too impatient and had everything to live for." Her eyes dimmed. "Have you met his wife, Ellie?"

"At the funeral," I said, recalling the bright and captivating woman I'd met in the receiving line a few hours before.

"Well, then you know what I'm talking about. We all love Ellie."

I set my still-full Coke on the table next to the couch and leaned forward, clasping my hands between my knees. "I get that. I do. But I'm still not clear on how I'm supposed to help. What exactly do you want me to do?"

Sarabella got to her feet, stepped in front of the massive stone hearth, and turned back with a sigh. "I have some questions—ones I can't look into myself—that I need you to investigate."

Shit. "What kind of questions?"

"Well, for starters, they're saying my son had a lot of enemies. That's news to me. Hell, some have even suggested that Ellie killed Don." She paused, clearing her throat. "Which may or may not be true."

I stared up at her. "But you just said you all love Ellie."

"We do love her. But that doesn't mean she didn't do it." Sarabella met my gaze head-on. "She has a motive and may have been the last person to see him alive. Then there's Dick Reardon. People are saying he did it because of some business difficulties. And he lives next door, which would be damned convenient. Then there's Charles Legro. He manages the new club in Sam's mansion. You know about it?"

"I've heard a little," I said. "But I left town before they bought the place."

"It's a big operation, Paul. It's operated by Societe Inter Nationale," she said, carefully emphasizing each word. "A French outfit. Put millions into renovating the place. You remember we all called Sam Norbeck's mansion the 'sin house' because he put his initials in large black iron letters on his ugly wrought iron front gate. *S. I. N.* A goddamned abomination. That's what it is. We all knew he did it just to piss off his neighbors, who he knew hated him. That was his sick sense of humor."

"We all got a laugh from it."

"Anyway, when they bought the place, they kept Sam's initials on the gate, so now we call it the Sin Club. And you better believe me, Paul, it is just that. It's gone rancid since I sold the house to them. You'll hear more about it after you've been here a few days. It's closed now for renovation, or I'd get you in there to look around. Legro and his thug, Gitano, are the only ones living there for the time being."

We were getting off the subject. Old Sam's mansion was beside the point.

"Sarabella," I said, "tell me a little more about Don's death. Why isn't it suicide?"

"Like I said, I've been told that Don had enemies."

"There has to be more to it than that."

"There is. Lots more. I'm not going to be here forever, and there are people in this town who think they're going to get some of my money when I go. Don was executor of my estate. You won't believe how that went down when I announced it. You'd have thought I'd given him carte blanche to rob the family blind."

"They could've trusted him," I said. "Everyone could've."

"Of course they could. He was the best of my three kids. Went the furthest. Was going to make something of himself. Married a great gal. Had an idea for a research company that was going to carry on some of old Sam's ideas. I was helping him."

"I didn't know that."

"Bertie and Susan have nothing to worry about. They should know they're secure."

I wasn't going to touch that one, another example of Norbeck family dysfunction. I moved on. "Okay. My next question: why pick me to investigate?"

"I'm coming to you because you aren't in line to inherit any of my money. You're the only one I can trust."

"Sarabella, I can't stay."

"You *have* to stay. I'm depending on you to find out who killed my son. I've invited people to dinner here tonight so you can get to know them. Each one knew Don, and each one could've killed him. Each had opportunity and motive to kill him. And one of them did it. I know it. It would've been so easy."

"I'm telling you this is something for the police, for professionals to look into, not a retired army officer."

Sarabella shook her head. "They're not going to look into it. They want to call it suicide. Their excuse will be that Don's father committed suicide, and sons of suicides often copy their fathers when they get stressed. They say this happens a lot. But I know Don was murdered—and I know you can find his killer."

"Look, I'm no detective. You need to hire a pro."

"I disagree," Sarabella said. She looked past me for a time before continuing. "I remember Don telling me about you looking into a Mafia money-laundering scheme in Akron a few years ago."

"I didn't do it willingly, and I really don't want to do it again." She had no idea how close I'd come to feeding the fishes in Biscayne Bay back then, and at the moment, I wasn't in the mood to tell her.

Her eyes closed, and the tears started. Then sobs. "Paul, I'm getting death threats now. I'm in danger."

I handed her a tissue and waited until she opened her eyes and looked at me. It gave me time to think about my answer. Enough time to cave.

"Okay, okay," I said. "One week. Only one week. Then I have to get back. I'm heading up a big machine installation for Henderson, and we're already behind schedule. One week max. Then I'm going back to Akron."

She turned off the faucet. The tears stopped, and her eyes opened wide. She dabbed at them with her hanky, and a faint smile replaced the gray that had been there. "You'll stay here. I have your room all set up."

I didn't answer.

"You can do it in a week. You're up to it." She smiled.

I thought for a minute, trying to frame my next question in such a way as to get an honest answer. I didn't want to upset her, but I needed an answer I could believe. "Maybe it was one of your kids. I know there was friction there. Any chance they could have done it?"

She glared at me for what felt like a full minute before she finally softened. "Neither of them did it. You can take it to the bank."

"You're certain?"

"Absolutely. They have their problems ... sure ... all siblings do. Susan has her emotional problems ... I know that, but she'll outgrow them."

"What about Bertie?"

"We sent Bertie to boarding school in Detroit, so naturally Detroit is where all his friends are. Grosse Pointe, Bloomfield Hills, up there. He doesn't know anyone here on Grosse Ile, so of course they talk about him. But, Paul, he's a good kid. They're both good kids. They never would've harmed a hair on Don's head. Don't even think about it. I adore them more than life itself."

I'd never heard her say that before.

She waited to let that sink in before continuing. "I adore them both despite what they may tell you. Susan is a wonderful person when you get past her hang-ups and her glamorous exterior. Men are taken in by those big blue eyes of hers. Bertie is just waiting to take on the responsibilities of family leadership. I'm sure they've told you I threaten them with disinheritance. But it's because I want them to face reality, to take a good look at what that world out there is really like. I've probably been doing it all wrong. It would all be so much better if Irwin were still here. I think they hate me and each other, despite what I've tried to do for them."

I wasn't going to touch that. I let her continue.

"I grew up poor, so I've never been sure of the best way to raise wealthy kids. They desperately needed a father, but they lost him before they were old enough to know him. They'll be taking on the family traditions and responsibilities after I pass on, but they're not ready to do it yet." She issued a soft sigh. "I don't deny Don was my favorite. I listened to him, and now Susan and Bertie are bitter that I made him executor of my estate with power of attorney." She sighed. "Paul, I have lots of money and am soon to die."

I said nothing. I wanted her to continue.

"Money destroys people," Sarabella said, looking away. "You have no idea how lucky you are not to have big money. It destroys ambition, the will to work—initiative. It corrodes their innards. It corrodes their mind. People become more concerned about losing what they have or what they expect to get than going out and earning themselves money of their own. They get impatient to get their share—what they think is their fair share. They're afraid I'll change my will, that they'll be cheated. They convince themselves they won't be able to survive without their share of the money—without inherited wealth. It becomes a sickness."

"But, Sarabella, lots of people cope well with the possibility of inheriting big money."

"And lots don't. Too many."

It was a long, sad story I already knew. More to the point, her soliloquy hadn't given me a single reason to exclude Bertie or Susan from the list of suspects. If anything, Sarabella's reflections on how money corrupts implicated her kids more than ever.

I thought it was time to change the subject. *Why is she avoiding what I've heard may be the real reason for his death?*

CHAPTER 6

DON'S BOOK

"What's this I hear about Don writing a book?"

Sarabella hesitated. She closed her eyes slowly, this time without the tears. Finally, she opened them and focused on me. "It was something Don was fooling with to kill time. Susan said something about it to me." She looked away, avoiding my eyes for a long moment.

I said nothing. Just waited.

Finally, without looking at me, Sarabella said, "Susan told me it was something I wouldn't like. I believe what she meant was I would *hate* it. Some kind of look into the Norbeck family archives."

"Don was very proud of what old Sam had done," I said. "Should be flattering."

"I wonder. I wish I knew."

"You want me to pursue it?"

She thought for a minute, then, still not looking at me, said, "Maybe you should. I understand it's on Don's computer. And somehow it's protected. By a password—or whatever. How, I have no idea. If it's so important that it has to be protected by a password, maybe there's something bad on it. Maybe there's something on that computer Don didn't want anyone to see. Maybe it's why Don was killed. I don't know. I'm only saying you should look for it."

"What if I find it?"

"If you get to the computer, destroy it—just to be safe. You don't need to look in it. If it's the reason Don was killed, you don't want to know what's in it. Could be dangerous."

"I'll look around."

"Don't look, Paul. Find it. Destroy it."

"Why? Aren't you a little curious about what's in it? Maybe Don found out more about your famous father-in-law. Maybe he found out who killed him. Shouldn't we look at it before destroying it?"

"Maybe it's about the Sin Club," she said quickly. "Maybe it's something they don't want us to know. A lot of bad stuff's happening there. You find out about it, and maybe they'll knock you off like Don."

"Are you saying those people killed Don?"

"Maybe. One possibility. A good one, in fact. You're going to find out. I'm merely saying the computer may be dangerous to have, and if so, better to just hit it with a hammer."

"You're not curious about it?"

"Paul, that Sin Club is out of control. They're doing bad things there they said would never happen. It's run by a man named Charles Legro."

"I saw him at the funeral. Didn't meet him."

"He's a Frenchman out of Paris. Dresses like a model for men's clothes. You must have seen that. I dealt with him when they were buying our mansion, and now I don't trust him. I don't believe a word he says anymore. You'll meet him tonight. I've invited him to the dinner. If the computer has anything about the Sin Club on it, it could be why Don was killed. You definitely want it destroyed. You don't want to know what's in it."

The room was silent for a long moment. I wondered about her logic. *Isn't there every reason to know what's on Don's computer?*

Then Sarabella said, "Maybe it involves Ellie."

"Ellie?"

"Yeah ... Ellie. She's told us almost nothing about her friends in New York. Almost nothing about what she did before she married Don. Maybe there's something there she doesn't want us to know."

"Maybe she's not the talkative type."

"Don told us she was involved with people with lots of money. Powerful people. Secret stuff. I don't know what."

I just listened. I hoped she would go on.

"So I had her checked out before the wedding and found out very little about her, nothing more than what Don told us. I learned she has a circle of wealthy friends in New York and that she knows very powerful people there, people I think may not necessarily allow the law to interfere with their activities. The first I met them was when we attended the wedding. As I got to know them, I realized they are unusually fond of her. They almost think of her as their daughter."

"What about her family? Did you meet them?"

"Her parents were there and seemed very nice, but they didn't say much about her."

"Did you ask?"

"When we asked, they were evasive, even about her job and what she was doing for a living. Ellie rarely mentions her family or even her hometown."

"I think I'm going to have to get to know Ellie before I believe any of that."

"All I'm saying is she's coming to dinner tonight, and she could've killed him. It's possible. Wait until you hear how he died."

"I already heard some of it," I said. "I guess she was there when his body was found."

"Yeah, but I'm not sure she can account for where she was before that, when Don died."

"I've also heard she's a lovely person, that everyone likes her. If she has rich friends in New York, why kill Don? For money?"

"I'm just saying," Sarabella said again, "she could've killed him. And if she did it, maybe it's because she didn't like what Don was putting on his computer. All the more reason to find the computer and destroy it."

I barely nodded. No way was I going to destroy that computer. "Okay, whatever." I waited a beat for emphasis. "But you know that only gets us partway. You can be sure the manuscript also resides on a backup hard drive somewhere. We have to find that computer and the backup and either very thoroughly erase the files or hammer both of them to pieces."

"I'm sure you can do it."

"And if someone did kill him and I start looking for who killed him, then I'm in deep shit like you."

She grinned. "Yeah. You probably already are."

"Like I said, I can only stay a week."

She said nothing.

After a long, quiet moment, I said, "What's this about you wanting me to stay *here*. I already checked in with Tom McGraw. I'll be staying there."

"That won't do. I want you to stay here—in this house."

"Oh, now wait a minute."

"You'll learn much more if you stay here. Second floor with connected bath. Beautiful room. Mattie'll show you."

I looked away.

"And, Paul, I'm so glad you're staying. I know you'll sort this whole thing out." Sarabella reached over to a button on a black box on the table next to her, and shortly, Mattie appeared.

"Yes, ma'am?"

"Paul is going to stay with us for a few days. Show him his room—you know, that front one I told you about."

"You mean next to Susan's room."

I winced. "Oh no."

"Hey, she's not here that much," Sarabella said quickly. "She won't bother you. Who knows, maybe you two will get back together."

"Not bloody likely."

"Oh, now goddamn it, Paul. Don't be like that. Get out of here and find me a killer."

Mattie looked at me, smiling a naughty smile, and motioned me with one finger to follow her.

When we were out of the room, I said severely, "Mattie, wipe that shit-eatin' grin off your face. Whatever you're thinking ain't going to happen."

As we started up the stairs side by side, she flashed that shit-eating grin at me one more time. "You'll be staying in the room at the top of the stairs. Where are your bags? I'll bring them up."

"No need, Mattie. I'll get it. Only one. I travel light. By the way, where does Bertie stay?"

"He's on the third floor. He has three rooms up there. One of them is his computer room. Won't let me in there. Only the good Lord knows what he does with all that stuff."

"He studied computers at MIT," I said, "so I imagine he wants to stay current."

We reached the top of the stairs, and I looked around the bed-sitting room Sarabella had selected for me. It was a large room, painted mostly white. Three windows with fancy lace curtains faced the river. A queen bed topped by too many pillows of every color was against one wall. Two large dressers, one with a mirror, stood against the wall opposite the bed. A small photo of Sarabella's three children rested in the lower left frame of the mirror. They were smiling. It had been taken years ago, before they became aware of the adult world and the tribulations that awaited them. On the other side of the room was a small table with knickknacks and a lamp that separated two stuffed chairs. It was too feminine for my taste, but I decided it would have to do.

I started to my car to get my things from Tom's apartment. "Thank you, Mattie. I'm going to enjoy my stay," I said, lying through my teeth, angry with myself for getting into this mess.

CHAPTER 7

SARABELLA'S DINNER PARTY

Thunder grumbled in the distance, and rain attacked the windows on the south side of the house as I walked down the stairs to Sarabella's living room. I thought it appropriate. All afternoon, I'd had a gut feeling that this wasn't going to go well.

At the center of it all stood Sarabella, in full charge, crystal wine glass in hand and flanked by the Reardons, daughter Susan, Ellie, and one newcomer whose eyes seemed fixated on Ellie's breasts. I could guess who he was. Bertie sat in a chair facing the hearth, gazing at a waning fire. To his right was a man behind a makeshift bar assembled from three folding card tables and covered in a white linen tablecloth, topped with an assortment of wine, liquor, and bottled water.

A catered event?

As soon as she saw me, Susan broke away from her mother and attached herself to me. "I know you miss Don as much as I do. I'm so sorry. I can't imagine life around here without him."

Sarabella soon noted my arrival, excused herself, and walked over.

"You're brave to do this so soon after, Sarabella," I said. "Thank you for including me."

"You had to be here, dear boy. You two were very close. I know you miss him."

"I do."

She gently unfolded Susan's arm from around mine, patted it twice, and looked up at me. "Come with me, dear. I don't think you know Charles

35

Legro." She led me over to a man of perhaps forty. As we approached, his eyes shifted to me. Susan followed us and smiled warmly at him.

He was slim and had black hair, graying at the temples, combed straight back and trimmed long and thick at the nape of his neck. His white, open-collared shirt, gold necklace and watch, and two-button medium blue sport coat over white pants was the uniform of the euro-riche. He had thin black eyes and a weak mouth that did not match his firm handshake.

"Paul, I want you to meet Grosse Ile's most distinguished resident. This is Charles Legro. His new club here on the island, Societe Inter Nationale, has put zest into our humble island community. We're famous around the world now."

"Good to meet you, Charles," I said, looking him in the eye, careful to pronounce his name "Charl." I was reminded once again that Sarabella could bullshit the best of them.

"Delighted to meet you, sir," he said in a deep voice with a trace of accent. "I understand you were close to Don. Sorry for your loss."

"Charles is a very busy man, Paul. Just being here is a real honor to Don."

Turning to Sarabella, he said, "My dear, I would never miss an invitation from you. And I must say, it's good to see you looking so well. We've all been very worried about you the past few days."

"I'm feeling better."

His eyes returned to me. "Will you be heading back to Akron soon? Sarabella tells me that's where you're working now."

"No. Sarabella insisted I stay on for several days. Maybe a week. I've been out of the country for three years and have some catching up to do. A lot of friends to see. I hear the island's changed since I've been away."

"Monsieur Legro," Sarabella said, gripping his arm above the elbow and looking to me, "has done an extraordinary job of bringing our simple village out of the last century to become one of the most prosperous towns in Michigan, perhaps the entire Midwest."

I wanted to look down to see if the manure had yet reached my knees.

"You're too kind, Sarabella," Charles Legro said, bowing slightly, still looking at me.

"No, really, Charles. This town has prospered like never before—and

I should know. My family here goes back to before Prohibition. Grosse Ile has been transformed. New streets, new airport—everything is new. We all thank you for what you've done for our community."

"Well, for me, it's been a pleasure. I'm so happy to have been a part of this renaissance."

Susan by now had moved close to Charles Legro. "Charles," she said, looking up at him, "it's been six days. How are things at the club?"

"Our renovation is on schedule, my dear. With a bit of luck, you should be back at the tables in a matter of weeks."

"I'll be back when this dreadful situation is behind us. Don was our love. It will take a while for me to recover."

"We all understand, of course. Come back when you're ready," Legro said as he looked down at his empty glass, then to the young man from the local country club before motioning for a refill.

Thirty minutes later, Sarabella announced dinner was served. We sauntered into the dining room, and like her affairs had always been in years past, and like Sarabella herself, the dinner-table setting was elegant. Mattie had brought out her best silverware and bone china.

Sarabella moved to the head of the table and motioned for me to sit to her right and Charles Legro to her left. Susan hurried to sit next to him. Ellie found a chair next to me and across from Susan. Bertie filed in and sat next to Ellie, followed by Dick Reardon at the far end of the table, facing Sarabella, and Anne next to him, facing Bertie.

A murmur of conversation continued for several minutes as we settled, then Sarabella spoke. "You're so kind to be here, everyone. There is a glass of champagne in front of each of you. I'd like you to stand for a moment and toast the life of a dear young man, cut short far too soon. Don would have wanted you all to enjoy the evening and celebrate his life. Please raise your glasses in his memory." Sarabella drained hers and motioned for another.

Dinner began with a delicious cup of lobster bisque.

"I can't believe such a nice man would do himself in," Anne Reardon said. "It just seems impossible."

"I had the impression he was under a lot of pressure," Dick said with a trace of a grin.

"But not that he would do this," Susan said.

Sarabella's eyes tracked from Anne to Dick to Susan.

"I was close to Don," Bertie said. "He could take it."

"Thank you for saying that, Bertie," Ellie said, looking down. "He was a loving guy and very devoted."

Sarabella glared at Dick.

"But he was under money pressure," Dick said. "His business wasn't going all that well. I know for a fact. That's all I meant."

"Trust me … *Dickie*," Bertie said, hesitating for effect, "Don had no money problems—nothing he couldn't handle."

Dick's face was red now, but he didn't reply.

After a long silence, Susan said brightly, "What a blessing it was for Societe Inter Nationale to come to Grosse Ile. We've all benefitted."

"I don't know," Bertie said. "I've heard rumors illegal aliens are coming into the country on Charles's boats."

"Not true, Bertie," Legro said, his voice an octave higher than usual. "You visit us from time to time. You ever see any?"

"I don't check passports when I visit. I wonder if you do."

"Bertie, you have no proof of that," Susan broke in. "It's very unfair of you to say it."

A sly smile on Dick Reardon's face suggested he wanted to say something, but before he did, Susan touched Legro's arm and looked into his eyes.

"Charles, don't take him seriously, for heaven's sake. That's just Bertie being Bertie. You know him. Always has to stir things up. He doesn't mean what he says."

She continued an animated conversation with Legro that I stopped listening to. Those baby blues of hers would keep Legro from standing up and leaving the room, which he had every right to do.

About then, Sarabella's caterer entered and served our dinner of filet mignon, baked potatoes, and salad. After Bertie's crack about Societe Inter Nationale, talk drifted away from Don to local events, the coming presidential election, and possible war in Palestine.

When dessert had ended, Ellie said, "Sarabella, the vanilla cheesecake was outstanding. And I just love the blue flower china—Wedgewood, right.? The cherry topping made it perfect."

Sarabella, looking down with eyes that told me she was wasted, barely nodded. She hadn't said a word after admonishing Bertie earlier in the dinner and had hardly touched her food. I recalled an old joke about shit hitting a fan.

Sarabella looked up from her plate and raised a hand for silence, her eyes inflamed. When we were quiet, her hand returned to the table and closed into a fist. "Now that you've all finished dinner, I want you to know I have a second reason for inviting you here tonight. I want to announce: Don was not a suicide."

Here it comes. Turn on the fan and duck.

Sarabella's eyes circled the table, stopping briefly to look directly at each of us for dramatic effect. Her hand was still a fist. She spoke in a low monotone. "That's right, everybody. Don was not a suicide. He was *murdered*." Sarabella glanced around the table again and continued. "Excepting my two beloved children, Bertie and Susan, and of course Paul here, who was in Akron when it happened, Don was murdered … by someone in this room."

"Not funny, Mother," Bertie stormed, a look of disgust on his face.

Legro looked up from the last of his dessert with a frown on his face, as if he hadn't heard correctly. Ellie also looked up, but was it alarm or puzzlement on her face? Susan shook her head slightly and smiled with an expression that said, "There goes Mother again." Then she looked down and returned to her dessert. By the time my eyes reached Reardon, he was forcing away a grin. Anne's face was blank, as if she hadn't heard.

Finally, Legro spoke in a calming voice. "Sarabella, I beg your pardon, but the police seem very sure of their opinion. How can you say such a thing of your friends in this room? We loved Don."

"I'm not exactly sure that's the case, Charles," Sarabella said, looking directly at him. "Each of you had a motive, and I can imagine how each of you could have done it." After the subdued groans of exasperation quieted, she continued. "For you, Charles, it would've been easy. You could've told your chief of security to do it. He'll do anything you ask. Ellie, you could have just popped him over the head and closed the garage door."

Ellie's face turned crimson.

Sarabella's gaze moved to Reardon. "You live next door to Don. You were home that day, cutting your lawn. You could've hit him over the head and closed the door. So could you," she said, shifting to Anne. "You could've walked over to his garage while he was working on his car. You knew of the difficulty your husband was having with Don. You only had to wait for him to turn his back."

Anne's deadpan look remained, and her attention returned to the dessert she hadn't touched.

"But, Sarabella, why would any of us have done such a thing?" Ellie said, both hands tightfisted on the table in front of her. "I had nothing against him. I loved him."

"You were fighting with Don, Ellie. You've already admitted you had a violent argument that day and had left Don and started home to New York. Besides, the money involved in Don's death is motive enough for anyone."

Ellie, a trace of fear in her eyes, did not reply.

Sarabella's attention returned to Reardon. "You were having serious arguments with Don over your business venture, and we all know Anne didn't like him. Reason enough." Then she looked to Legro. "Susan tells me you were scared of the book he was writing. I'm sure you wanted it stopped."

Legro carefully put his spoon down and looked at her for a few seconds. "Sarabella, I'm not going to dignify your speculation with a denial. Let me just say that there are rumors suggesting that vicious, untrue stories, deeply disturbing to a number of powerful interests, are contained on the late Mr. Norbeck's computer. If they were to be revealed, deep wounds could be inflicted in the hearts of powerful interests. The only reason there has not been more violence is because the computer's password disappeared with the unfortunate death of Mr. Norbeck." His eyes moved first to Bertie, then to me, as he continued. "I urge each of us at this table to allow the password to be buried with Mr. Norbeck."

No one said anything for what seemed like minutes. No one moved in their chairs. Bertie continued to stare at Sarabella with a look of disgust on his face.

Finally, Dick Reardon leaned forward. "You're quite right, Sarabella. I was there, cutting my lawn, just as you said—with my eyes wide open. And I'm here to tell you, in complete honesty, before God and country, that I did not kill your son. He had visitors that day, though. If it *was* murder, I can tell you who did it."

Anne turned to him. "I've heard you say some stupid things, Dick, but that may take the cake."

Charles Legro stared at her.

Reardon, scowling, swung his head around to her. "Anne, if you can't say something intelligent, shut that stupid mouth of yours. How would you know what I saw?"

Anne looked down at her dessert and started to dab at it with her spoon. Legro continued staring at her.

Apparently not wanting to make the situation any worse than it was with her accusations of premeditated murder and Dick Reardon's savage insult, Sarabella said nothing more on the subject of her son's murder—or any subject, for that matter—and turned her attention to her dessert that up to now she hadn't touched. Next, she plunged into the champagne. No one else said anything either.

One by one, everyone folded their napkins, rose from the table, thanked Sarabella for a fine meal, and moved back to the living room for some "after dinners" that no one needed, and normal conversation gradually resumed. It appeared everyone had silently concluded that Sarabella had had more to drink than she should've and was just venting her rage and sorrow over the loss of her son.

Charles Legro was the first to leave, saying Eric was waiting for him with the car. Soon after, Reardon rose from his chair and announced, "Sorry to leave so early, everyone, but I've lots to do tomorrow, and it looks like the rain has stopped." He walked over to me, gripped my arm, and said, "Paul, could you help me find my raincoat? I left it in one of the guest rooms. You know your way around this place better than me."

"Sure," I said, getting to my feet.

When we were out of the room, he said, "You have any idea about the business Don and I were in here in town?"

"Not really. Don never said anything to me about it. It all started while I was away."

Reardon said nothing more until we reached the guest room where the coats lay on a bed. We entered, and Reardon closed the door.

"Those people don't need to hear this," he said. "Don had come up with an idea for a computer application to improve automobile highway navigation, and he needed my help. It turns out Don needed *a lot* of my help. In fact, he was in over his head when he asked me to join his company. As a matter of fact, he was a fucking mess. I think he was writing a tell-all book about his family and planned to use it to squeeze more money out of Mama. Keep this under your hat, of course. No need for anyone to hear it."

"Of course not."

"I'm working our way out of trouble now, but there's lots more to do. When he died, it was getting to the point where I was keeping him around just to keep the door open for more of Sarabella's money. As you can imagine, she's a bitch to work with. Has no idea what business is all about."

I just listened.

He found his raincoat and started to put it on. "And now you've met Ellie."

I nodded.

"What a doll," he said. "Don was in way over his head with her too."

"I can't believe it."

"Couldn't manage her. And his temper was driving them apart real fast, to the point she was coming on to me. I could understand, of course, but I had to push her away to keep access to Mom's money. It's a very delicate situation. You understand."

"I can imagine. But why are you telling me this?"

He gripped my arm again and pulled me closer. He looked around, then spoke directly into my ear. "I heard Sarabella has you checking into this. I'm here to tell you it was one ugly situation before Don died."

"Sounds like it," I said. "Sounds like you've got a problem keeping Anne in line too. You don't want her finding out about you and Ellie."

He shook his head. "Oh hell, no problem there. That dimwit couldn't figure her way out of a paper bag wide open at one end."

I finally asked him the obvious question: "Did you really see who killed Don?"

"I got a pretty good idea. He had visitors that afternoon. Coulda been murder. Coulda not been murder." He was still speaking directly into my ear. "Like Sarabella said, I was cutting my lawn when it happened. Come over to the house some evening, and I'll tell you all about it."

"How about right now?"

"Too complicated. High finance. You know. Besides, let's face it, I'm shit-faced." He released my arm. "Give me a call and come over some evening. Soon."

"I'll do that."

By now, he had located Anne's raincoat, opened the guest room door, and headed out to find Anne and leave. Anne was at the front door, waiting for him to open it. He walked to the door and then stopped, looked back, and winked at me. "Call first." Reardon then gave the raincoat to Anne, opened the door, and pushed her out.

CHAPTER 8

MATTIE'S CONCERN

It had been a long day, but it turned out the evening was not yet over. The guests were gone now, and the house was still. Sarabella had headed off to bed, and Susan and Bertie had disappeared into their rooms. I'd gone to my room to do some unpacking and stash supplies in dresser drawers and bathroom shelves. I was feeling a little better now. Every room in the house brought back good memories of my visits to Don, and this room was no exception.

Mattie appeared at the door. "I saw your light was still on. Anything I can get for you before bed?"

"Nothing I can think of for now," I said. "And I have to say, you performed a miracle tonight. Everything was superb."

Her smile vanished. She waited a few seconds to gather her thoughts, looked each way down the hall, then entered the room and closed the door without a sound. There was a serious look on her face as she walked up to me. "You have time for some talk?"

"For you, always. What's it about? Sarabella?"

"I'm not going to talk about Sarabella. What I'm going to say is that I wish you hadn't agreed to look into this."

"I didn't want to," I said as I continued unpacking. "Sarabella insisted. She really leaned on me."

"We should let Don rest in peace. If you get into this, you'll be in as much danger as he was. I don't want to see that. Better to let things alone. Let his book die."

I stopped unpacking, straightened up, and looked at her. "Why's that? What's this all about?"

"Paul, the Norbeck family has black secrets that must not see the light of day. They *must* stay where they're buried."

"What are they? Can you tell me?"

"No. Not even you. That's all I'll say." Mattie looked down at the floor, then back up. "I believe Don had uncovered these secrets and put 'em in his book. That's why he's dead. I'm sure of it. Someone found out he put 'em in his book. And now you have to find his book. And destroy it. That's all you have to do this week. Nothing more. Don't read the book. Don't think about it. Just find the book and destroy it. The Norbeck secrets must die with Don. And stay dead." There was a look of dread on her face for what seemed over a minute. Then she turned, opened the door, and without another word left the room.

I was exhausted and confused. What the hell had I gotten myself into? I closed the door, showered, worked my way into shorts, turned down the bed, turned off the lights, and fell in. I had buried my head in the pillow and was close to the dead sleep of the totally exhausted when the far side of the bed moved lightly and a form slid in beside me.

I was very tired. I desperately wanted it to be my imagination.

CHAPTER 9

AN INVITATION TO SIN

I didn't have to open my eyes. The perfume gave her away.
"Susan."

"Of course, darling," she purred as she rolled over to me and put a hand on my shoulder.

"Susan, get out of here. Get the hell out of here." I meant it and didn't whisper. It looked like I was going to have to be the one with the self-discipline.

"Darling," she said, "I'm lonely, and I want to talk."

"I'm dead tired, not lonely, and can't talk," I said in almost a whisper. I didn't move my head from the pillow. "Whatever it is can wait till morning."

"Sweetheart, you'll want to hear what I have to say."

"Why in the world would I want to hear what you have to say at this godforsaken hour?"

"If you're serious about looking into Don's suicide …"

I rolled onto my back and looked up at the blackness. I didn't say anything for a minute or more. I was thinking this was not going to end well.

"Okay," I said. "We'll just talk."

"Not just yet. I'm not really in the mood to talk."

I rolled farther over and looked. Even in near total darkness, I could see that Susan wasn't dressed for conversation. She was sitting up, and what little she did have on was white and slowly slipping off a shoulder, the one that still had something on it. The other shoulder was bare, as was most of what was below it. What every twelve-year-old boy dreamed of was about to happen—an attack by a raving nymphomaniac with all the passion of a convicted murderer sentenced to die the next morning.

Okay, so I was shameless—also weak. I would do better tomorrow. But for now, all the self-discipline I liked to think I had was gone. So I rationalized: I owed it to Sarabella to find out all I could about Don's death. This would be just another of the many sacrifices I made in the pursuit of justice.

"Let me help you with that heavy weight on your shoulder," I said, "so it will be easier for you to talk."

I needn't have suggested it. She was in my arms now, completely out of whatever she had on when she walked in, and struggling to help me out of my shorts. For at least the next three-quarters of an hour—I wasn't counting—little of our conversation made much sense.

I finally whispered, "Susan, time to come up for air," and rolled her off me.

For several minutes, we both looked up at the blackness. Finally, I said, "Now, did you really have anything important to say?"

"Let me think, darling." She didn't move for at least a minute before saying, "Oh yeah—I remember now. Yes, I did. As a matter of fact, it has to do with why you're here. If you're serious about checking into Don's death, there are some things you need to know."

"Please believe me. I'm not serious about looking into Don's death. Suicide works for me, if that's what the police want to believe. This is all your mother's idea. She's the one who thinks Don was murdered. But if you have something to tell me, go ahead. Suppose you tell me all about your mom's guests at dinner tonight. She thinks one of them killed Don."

"Oh, Mom's hysterical. That's all it is. She just doesn't want to believe there's another suicide in the family."

"You have to admit she was right about motives and opportunities. Tell me why Dickie Reardon didn't kill him."

"Reardon's an oversized ass, but he's not a killer. He's a phony. He couldn't kill anyone. He thinks Ellie is in love with him. Hell, she can't stand even being around him. Did you see her anywhere close to him tonight? I can't stand being near him either. He makes my skin crawl. He lives in a dream world, for God's sake."

"So why did Don get involved with him in his new business?"

"Don wanted to explore some ideas he found in Grandpa Sam's notes when he was starting his research into the family archives and needed floor space and equipment in the Detroit area. Reardon has a fairly extensive machine shop just south of Detroit with office space Don needed. He offered help. Now he thinks Don's ideas were all his own and it was him pulling Don up by his bootstraps. It's all in his mind. All bullshit. In the past several months, Don had figured out the deal with Reardon wasn't working and was trying to separate from him."

"There you go. Motive for Reardon to kill him."

"Anyone but Reardon. He hasn't got it in him. He's just a windbag."

"So, if not Reardon, what about Ellie? She could have popped him, then gone to the police and asked them to intervene."

"I know Ellie. You don't. She couldn't have done it. She loved Don, despite what anyone says. No motive. No way she needs the money."

"Then there's Monsieur Charles Legro to consider. Maybe he did it or had his friend Gitano do it."

"You know anything about the Sin Club?"

"I believe sin is mentioned in the Bible."

"By sin, *dear*, I mean Societe Inter Nationale. We call it the Sin Club."

"Sounds sexy. Does it live up to its name? I can't believe it's any kind of big deal."

"You're going to hear a lot about it in the coming days. Some of the stories are going to be very lurid—and very exaggerated."

"Should I believe any of them?"

"Believe less than half," she said.

"Why less than half? I hear it lives up to its nickname."

"They should've taken Grandpa's initials off that gate. It was a big mistake leaving them there. That's the only reason for its bad reputation. You'll see for yourself."

"How? It's closed for weeks. You can't even get in. Legro said so tonight."

Her face brightened to a smile. "Not so. Tuesday, you're going to see for yourself, my dear. Before he left tonight, he invited us to a private dinner at his club. Just us two. Insists you be there. And before dinner, he's going to show you around the club."

"How'd you arrange *that*?"

"I didn't. It was his idea."

"I hear you can go anytime."

"Anytime. We Norbecks all have memberships. It was part of the deal when they bought the place from Sarabella. Sometimes I go there with Bertie. He loves the place."

A moment of silence intervened before Susan, still on her back beside me, spoke again.

"I've gotten to know Charles. He's a fine man. He's a gentleman and a very nice guy. He's internationally known and brings the best people from around the world to our little island to enjoy a world-class club. I've met many of his friends."

"Looks European cool to me."

"You'll like him when you get to know him. He knows everybody—everywhere. Right at home in the top cities of the world. London. Paris. Tokyo. You name it."

"I wonder if he's at home in some of the cities I got to know—intimately. Baghdad, Mosul, Kabul, Fallujah."

"Maybe not. Why would he?"

"I can assure you it would round out his education."

"He doesn't need more education."

"When I met him tonight at dinner, to be honest, I thought he did. If he's so international, why pick little old Grosse Ile for his casino?"

"I already asked him that. He says he likes the privacy."

Without saying another word, Susan gathered her negligee, threw it over her shoulder, jumped off the bed, walked to the door, slammed it, and was gone.

CHAPTER 10

SARABELLA IS UNDER THE WEATHER

Breakfast the next morning began for me when I entered the Norbeck dining room, looked at my watch, and saw that it was 9:17 a.m. Susan and Bertie were already there, and Susan motioned for me to sit next to her at the table. Bertie was standing at the buffet, meticulously fussing with the components of a breakfast he was preparing on a tray. His back was to us, and he did not turn around when I entered.

As I seated myself, Bertie said, "Mother isn't coming down for breakfast."

"What?" I said.

Without turning his head, Bertie said, "Last night may have been one too many for her. After the party, I got her a cup of coffee and helped her up to bed. She fell getting into bed. She didn't break anything, but she's got a splitting headache this morning. When I asked her what happened, she didn't make much sense. She's having trouble keeping anything down, so I'm making a light breakfast for her."

Other than the funeral, it had been a long time since I'd seen Bertie. In all the years I'd hung out with Don at the Norbecks, I'd never gotten to know him. He was never home, and as a result, he knew almost no one on Grosse Ile. His friends, if he had any, were fellow students from Detroit or elsewhere. I would see him occasionally on holidays when Don said he hadn't been able to inveigle a stay with school friends.

His name was really Albert, but Bertie fit him better. His parents

50

must have thought so too, because that's what they'd always called him as long as I could remember. When I did see him, he always made me feel uncomfortable. I guess because he seemed very smart. A lot smarter than me. He once said his sister and brother and all their friends bored him because they were stupid.

I always thought of him as a geeky kind of guy. Bertie was over six feet in height, pear shaped, and soft and pudgy with light brown, curly hair he never combed, cut longer than I ever would have wanted. He'd always left me uninterested in ever getting to know him. On the other hand, I must say he was always cordial to me. But that was as far as it went.

"Sleep well, my darling?" Susan asked.

"The sleep of the dead," I said as I slipped into the chair next to her.

"I didn't know what you would want for breakfast. Mattie can get you anything. Help yourself to what's on the table: toast, coffee. There's orange juice too."

"Four eggs scrambled and fries work for me," I said, glancing at Susan. "Exercise before bed always gives me an appetite at breakfast."

Bertie looked back at us with a quick smile, then went back to his ministrations. Susan nudged up to me, and her hand slipped to my thigh under the tablecloth overhang. Breakfast was going to be, shall we say, stimulating.

"We've been talking about what's going to happen to our inheritance now that Don's gone," Susan said. "I was telling Bertie that after Ellie gets her share, the rest of it would be split between us. He doesn't think so."

"So how else?" I asked as I reached for the marmalade.

"Actually, he thinks Don was getting the whole thing, and now Mother will find a way to screw him out of his share and give it all to me or maybe charity. He thinks she's going to frame him for Don's murder." She sounded rather pleased about it.

Bertie broke in without looking back. "Susan, for God's sake, Paul doesn't need to hear that. There're all kinds of rumors floating around now. That's only one. Mother's all over the place. Let's face it, it's no secret she hates my guts. Keeps saying I should get my ass out of the house and get a job."

"She doesn't hate your guts," Susan said. "Besides, what's wrong with you getting a real job? For Christ's sake, you're thirty-five years old and still living at home."

"I've told you twenty times that would be ridiculous. Sure, I could get a job, but with all our money, what's the use?"

"I've never heard you say anything as stupid as that," I said.

"You're not around here that much. Stick around. You'll see what I'm talking about."

"Bertie, I know it's none of my business, but you really have to get over this 'Mother hates me' shit."

"You're right about one thing. It *is* none of your business. She's been on my back my whole life. You've heard her tell me she's going to screw me out of my money any number of times, and Susan too. She says it all the time. 'Get off your ass and get a job,' she says."

"So she wants you employed like the rest of the world," I said. "She wants you to make something of yourself. Is that all bad?"

Now he turned to face us. "Is it at all *necessary*? Tell me that. We got old Sam's money now. We don't need to work. Leave the jobs to people who need jobs. Why should I take a job someone else really needs?"

"She just wants what's best for you," Susan said. "She wants you gainfully employed. Maybe you could start up a company and actually create more jobs for people."

"She'll put me on the street if she has to."

"There're worse things in life," I said. "I'm on the street, as you put it, and I'm surviving."

"She'd frame me for Don's murder if she thought it would light a fire under my ass," he said, a weak smile across his face.

"So you think it was murder too."

"Yeah," he said with an attitude implying the question was dumb. "It has to be. Don wouldn't do that to himself. Just because Dad did it doesn't mean Don did. That's an old wives' tale that kids follow their dads who kill themselves. Hell, we're not even that sure Dad killed himself."

"That's bullshit, and you know it," Susan said. "We know he did it."

"Can't be absolutely sure. Someone killed Grandpa Sam. Maybe the same guy has it in for our family. Who the hell knows?"

"You're full of shit," Susan said.

Tired of the bickering, I said, "Knock it off, guys. Change the subject."

Bertie said, "Paul, I have to take this tray up to Mother, but later, meet me in my room. It's on the third floor. You may find I'm not quite as full of shit as Susan thinks." With that, he picked up the tray, steadied it, and marched out of the room and up the stairs.

By now, Susan's hand was all over my thigh to the point that I wasn't going to stand up and reach for more coffee or anything else anytime soon. "Susan, reach over and pass the coffee. Maybe one more cup will calm me down."

"By all means, darling," she said with a satisfied grin.

Mattie entered the room, and Susan's hand jumped off my thigh. Mattie set a plate of scrambled eggs and fries down in front of me.

"Mattie, you're a mind reader. How did you guess?"

Mattie smiled, looked at both of us, and said, "I've been listening in." Then she collected the used dishes and left.

I looked at Susan. "When did Bertie come down with all this crap about Sarabella wanting to frame him for murder? Is he losing it?"

"It's been building since Don's death, but I think it was Mother's performance last night at dinner that put it over the top. He's spending way too much time in that computer room of his. He's in there all the time."

"Yeah. What about his computer room?"

"He has one whole bedroom full of computers, screens, wires, you name it. It's crazy. He won't let me near it. He locks the room when he's away. Sounds like he wants to show it to you."

"I'll be fascinated. Hope he does."

Susan pouted momentarily. Then her face brightened. "You'll be more fascinated with what I have for you next Tuesday at the Sin Club, my love." Her hand was back on my thigh.

CHAPTER 11

BERTIE'S COMPUTER ROOM

Bertie motioned for me to come in. Just as Susan had said, computers, computer screens, recording devices, and every conceivable device that went with them were connected by wires and scattered about the room. There were cables everywhere. A powerful telescope pointed out of a north-facing window in the general direction of Detroit, barely visible in the distance to the north. Attached to the telescope's eyepiece was a black box that I assumed gathered and recorded information from the telescope and transferred it to an Apple laptop on one of the workbenches.

"What's so interesting about Detroit?" I asked, gesturing to the telescope.

"It's not pointed at Detroit. It's looking at Societe Inter Nationale next door. Look down. It's about three hundred yards away."

On closer inspection, I saw the telescope was indeed pointed too low to see Detroit. "But you can't put much of a file together just by looking at the club from here."

Bertie smiled. "The receiver attached to this telescope can see in the dark. It detects infrared light. I can see them bring their boats in, unload people, then reload their customers and take them home. In daylight, this thing can get me close enough to recognize their faces. The people they bring in are from all around the world: Canada, South America, Europe, Asia, you name it."

"But how can you know where they come from just by looking?"

"I don't *just* look. I hear. These computers hack their computers and their security network. When I listen in, which isn't often because I don't

54

want them catching on, I can see and hear everything that goes on. I placed bugs in their office, their party rooms, and upstairs bedrooms when I visited a while back. There's damn little they can do that I don't know about. You won't believe what they're getting away with."

This guy needs a life, I thought. *He spends all his time spying on his next-door neighbor. With his brain, he should be in the CIA. He needs a tour of duty in the army. Anything to get him off his ass in his room with the door closed.*

"I'm going to show you something I've only ever shown to the late great Don Norbeck," he said. "And it's with the understanding that you keep it to yourself. You *will not* tell a soul. If certain people find out you know what I'm going to tell you, you'll end up like Don. You have to keep this to yourself."

I got it now. He's living in a parallel universe. All by himself.

"What's the big deal?" I said, bending down to get a close look at Bertie's installation. "That club is legit. Susan told me so last night."

"Susan is clueless. They're playing her like a Stradivarius. She's there all the time but only in the dining room, the gambling tables, and the second- and third-floor party rooms. They keep her away from the bad stuff. And I keep her away from this room."

I stopped looking around at the computers. "Then why show me? Why do I need to know?"

"Mom asked you to look into Don's death and said you're serious about it."

"Well, I agreed to look into it, but I'm not sure what I can do. I'll check in with the cops and maybe talk with Ellie. But there's not much else I can do. I have to be back home next week. What can I find in a week with the coroner saying it's suicide?"

"When you see what I've got here, you'll have a lot to check out."

I don't want a lot to check out. "Show me," I said, looking around. "I'm amazed at your setup."

"You're going to have to swear to keep it quiet. You can't say a thing to anyone about what I'm going to show you. I'm deadly serious. It's life or death. For me and you. When I tell you, you'll know why."

I looked around again and nodded. "Okay. I agree. All this stays in my head unless you say otherwise."

Bertie motioned me to a chair in front of a large computer screen. "I've been monitoring the Sin Club for about two years now. It's a nasty piece of work. They're doing a beautiful job of keeping it quiet, but it turns out those guys are animals. Don was interested too. I guess you know he was writing a book."

"Yeah, Sarabella told me. She thinks there's something bad in it. Doesn't say what. Wants me to destroy the computer."

"Could be about Societe Inter Nationale. They've taken Grandpa's mansion and turned it into a whorehouse."

"A whorehouse?"

"Sure. It's small and compact compared to similar commercial clubs in Las Vegas and Europe like the Playboy Mansion but far more exclusive and particular about who is invited to join. They have world-class dining and gambling. It's closed now for renovation but otherwise open seven days a week. Legro lives there on the third floor with his valet/bodyguard, Eric Gitano. He's there all the time. She may think Don put something about it in his book." Bertie let that soak in for a moment.

I waited.

"You remember when Sam owned the place?"

"Sure."

"There wasn't all that much to do on the third floor, was there?"

"Only bedrooms and baths, as I remember."

"Well, they've totally renovated it, opened part of it up so you can see down to the first floor, and even added an oversized, glassed-in elevator."

That I've got to see. "Must've cost a few bucks."

"You remember the two boat wells for Grandpa's powerboats—the ones he loved to experiment on?"

"Yeah. I hear they're bigger now."

"*I guess so.* They can put sixty-eight-foot Sunseekers in 'em now."

"What the hell's a Sunseeker?" I didn't want to sound stupid, but I had to ask.

Bertie looked at me for a beat. "Sunseekers are super-sleek yachts the size of World War Two PT boats, except they're faster. They pick up billionaires from Canada and as far away as Cleveland for a fast boat ride to their club and lots of fun and games on the way. It's a fun ride for those people and even more fun when they get there. They keep a jet at the airport. It'll hold eight people."

"Okay, so what's the big deal? Good food and gambling are available around the world."

"Remember how we all looked for Sam's safe room?"

"Sure."

"We never found it, did we?"

"No."

"They did!" Bertie looked as if he'd discovered the Hope Diamond.

"There really is one?"

"Yeah. Turns out it was well hidden, and no one could find it until some experts used instruments."

"What's it like?"

"It's large, beautifully laid out. Sam could have lived in it for a month without anyone knowing he was there. Had a kitchen, good-sized living room, and a small bedroom."

I wondered how in hell we could have missed it. "So, what are they doing with it now? I suppose it's wide open now to show the members."

"Au contraire, mon ami. Just the opposite. Still secret. They deny there ever was such a room. Show only very special, very high-paying guests."

"Why secret?"

"Because now they have some very special fun and games going on in it. I call it their sickroom."

"Their what?"

"You don't need to know."

"That bad, eh?"

"That bad. Just think the worst you can think of. Then double it."

What could he be thinking? I knew Bertie wasn't thinking of Iraq. He'd never been there—never seen real evil in all its variants. "How the hell do you know all this?"

"I got it on digital."

I sat back in my chair. I didn't believe it. *This guy definitely needs to get out of his room and see the world. Is he dreaming this? A visit to the real world would really help. Maybe meet some women. He could come to Akron. I could fix him up. Maybe he should travel.* Finally, I said, "Show me."

"I can't."

"Why not?" *When he tells me it's his inner voices, I'm out of here.*

Bertie slowly shook his head. "Paul, this is major Mafia shit. I'm not going to touch it. Word gets out …"

"What?"

"I die—badly."

"Tell the police."

"They'd put me in jail for recording this shit. Besides, don't you suppose the cops are in on it? How could this keep going if they weren't looking the other way? Don't you suppose the cops can figure out where the money for their new station came from? Where the money for all these new streets, schools, and the airport came from? Do you really think they give a shit about what's going on? Gimme a break."

"So go to the feds."

"One word leaks out—and it will—I'll get fed to their dog food machine."

"Excuse me?"

"The dog food machine."

"Say it again."

"You haven't heard of the dog food machine?"

"No. Sorry."

"You lived here how long and haven't heard of the dog food machine? In Detroit? That story's been around since Prohibition."

"Tell me about it."

"Goes back to the twenties, maybe before that. Rumor was that whenever a well-known hood disappeared in Detroit, housewives noticed their little puppy dogs began to go nuts over local canned dog food."

"Come on, Bertie. That's got to be bullshit." I stood up from my chair and pushed it back.

"Bullshit? Who knows, but it's known that canned dog food is made up of junk animal carcasses. All kinds, sizes, and shapes. They put them through a huge chopping machine that breaks up meat, bones, skulls, intestines. You know, trash flesh. The machine turns it into a mush. Then they add flavoring and vitamins and feed it through an extruder into cans. The cans are sealed and labeled and sent on to local grocery stores. No reason a human body or two can't be added to the chopping machine from time to time for flavoring. Maybe even alive. Why not? They say that's where Jimmy Hoffa ended up."

"I don't believe it."

"Hey, I can't prove it, but any housewife will tell you little Muffie will go nuts if she doesn't get canned dog food after people go missing in Detroit."

"Come on—"

"This much we know. Happened not long after Hoffa disappeared."

I shook my head, looked for a chair by the window, and sat down. *Does Bertie really believe this? Sometimes MIT graduates get weird, particularly if they spend too much time in their rooms.*

Bertie looked at me and smiled for a long moment. He was silent. Then he was serious. "Paul, leave Don to the professionals. Get your ass back to Akron."

CHAPTER 12

INTERVIEW

I didn't follow Bertie's advice. Instead, I phoned the Grosse Ile Police Department and asked if there was someone there I could talk to about the Don Norbeck death.

The voice on the phone got right to the point. "Who's speaking?"

"My name is Steiger. Paul Steiger. I'm calling at the request of Mrs. Sarabella Norbeck."

"Just a minute, sir."

After a long wait, the phone clicked, and a voice said, "Sir, this is Sergeant LaGrange. Would this be the Paul Steiger I knew from way back?"

"Yes, it is," I said, relieved that the process of interviewing the police would be with a guy I'd known for years, since I was in grade school and he was a big deal on our football team. He didn't know who I was then, but I looked up to him. He graduated, never quite made it to college, and stumbled around for a while, not sure what he wanted to do until signing up with the Grosse Ile Police Department. It wasn't long after I started driving a car that he stopped me for speeding and let me off with a warning. Then, after I went off to college, I would bump into him during summer vacations at Moorey's Grove, and we got to know each other a little better.

"Long time no see," I said.

"That's certainly true. What can I do for you?"

"I'm calling to find out if there's any way I could get some information about Don Norbeck's death. I happen to be in town for his funeral, and I'm hoping to get a feel for how he died."

"As a matter of fact, it turns out the chief just now authorized me to fill you in on details. It seems Sarabella Norbeck is making trouble, and he thinks perhaps you could help calm her down if you knew some of the details we know. Would you be interested in coming over now so I could fill you in?"

"By all means. It would be great to see you again."

"I'll be here. Got some pictures and a preliminary report to show you."

It took me fifteen minutes to get there, and another ten or so to get through the electronic security system that kept the main door locked until it was satisfied I was honest and unarmed. Sergeant Chuck LaGrange met me on the other side of the door, checked me through security, and silently motioned for me to follow him to his office. He was still the guy who threw footballs and won games for us—tall, slimmer than I would have thought for a guy his age, with short blond hair still not showing so much as a trace of gray. He had a flat gut and the same round, rugged face with small, sharp, wide-set, observant gray eyes over a nose that had seen one too many impacts with opposing linemen.

He led me down a long hall of highly polished linoleum and freshly painted walls. It smelled clean and a little like leather. We proceeded past doors identified with official-sounding titles in block letters until he opened the last of them and we walked into his office. Files and eight-by-ten crime-scene color photos all neatly squared up were arranged on his desk. An eight-foot-long table on one side of the room was cluttered with more files and pictures. Before he sat, he asked if I could use a coffee. I said no. He pointed me to one of the chairs opposite his desk. We sat down, and he looked at me intently for a long moment.

"What have you heard so far about Don's death?" he asked.

"I hear they're saying it was suicide and that Mrs. Norbeck doesn't believe it. As a matter of fact, I don't either."

"What else?"

"That someone unknown hit him over the head, started up the car engine, and closed the garage door."

"Anything else?"

"Sarabella thinks any number of people could have done it and had motives to do so. She can't understand why it's being called a suicide."

"Sounds pretty close to what we've heard's being said."

"So why the suicide verdict?"

"Not necessarily a verdict, Paul. Let's just say at this point it's a widely held suspicion. When you see what I'm going to show you, I think you'll see why we're leaning to suicide. The chief authorized me to show you all this, hoping you'll go back to Mrs. Norbeck and explain it to her—calm her down."

"First, you'll have to convince me it's suicide."

"Understood. I'll do my best."

"I've known Don since we were kids," I said, "and I can't imagine him killing himself. He was very positive toward life. So give me your best shot."

Chuck stood up. "Let me show you some photos taken up close and personal."

He walked around his desk and led me over to the table on which there were arranged color photos taken when the police first arrived at the Don Norbeck residence. I took a long time looking at each of the photos and opening the files and glancing through them. The gut burn was back. Heavy-duty. Then I went over to his desk and went through what was there.

"Don is lying on his side on the floor beside a workbench in his garage in those photos," Chuck said. "The hood of his car is up. An automobile transmission dipstick is on the floor beside him next to some broken glass. An open can of transmission oil had tipped over on the table. Oil had spilled from it onto the table and to the floor."

I closed my eyes and took a deep breath to give me some time to push aside the vision of Don's head on his garage floor. "What the hell is that all about?"

"We think Don was checking his transmission when he decided to kill himself." Chuck gave me time to absorb it all and then motioned me back to my chair. "Don's wife said they'd had an argument, as they often did from what we know from past reports, and she made the decision to go to her home in New York City. She packed a suitcase and drove her car to Detroit Metro Airport. There she bought a ticket and was waiting for her flight when she had a change of heart, canceled the ticket, and returned home. Before arriving home, she thought it prudent to stop here to request an officer follow her home because she thought Don would still be belligerent. I was the officer who followed her home."

"You were the one who found him in the garage."

"Yes. She checked the upstairs bedrooms and asked me to check the garage. He was pretty much as you see him in the photos. The car engine was still running."

"Yeah, but why would he do it while working on his car?"

"It looked to me as if he became despondent when his wife left him, closed the garage door, got in his car, and started the engine. After a period of time, he slumped against the car door. It opened. He fell out, staggered to his workbench, knocked over the oil, and fell to the floor, hitting his head. It was not a fatal head injury, but with all the carbon monoxide in the garage, particularly at ground level, it probably was enough to cause him to lose consciousness."

"This means he changed his mind. He didn't commit suicide. It was accidental death."

"Doesn't work. He didn't change his mind because he didn't turn off the motor. There was a door opener on the wall. He went by it and didn't push the button. He had a remote garage door opener in his pocket. He didn't use it to open the door."

"I notice in this one picture broken glass on the floor. What's that about?"

"You may have noticed in one photo an open can of Coke there on the bench. Don was probably drinking it from a glass. It apparently got pushed to the floor when Don slipped and tried to right himself as he fell. You'll notice in this close-up of Don's head, the pink cast to his skin. This is always the case in carbon monoxide deaths."

"I understand the coroner looked at him a couple of days ago. What did he have to say?"

"It was a quick look, and it appeared to him like a typical suicide."

"Autopsy?"

"He hasn't said so."

"Anything else?"

"He found other bruises on Don's body, but they were older bruises. So far, they're unexplained. They do not seem to pertain to the death." Chuck let all this sink in for a time. "I have to tell you, Paul, the chief believes it was suicide. We're not doing anything more on the case, pending release of the official coroner's report. He reminds us that Don's father committed suicide many years ago and that it's not uncommon for children of suicides to use that same mechanism as a solution to their problems."

"Don didn't have those problems. He loved life." A deep pit of remorse had returned to my gut, and I took some time to get up from my chair and look at the photos again. I refused to believe a close friend like Don could do this. It didn't make sense. I kept looking at the photos and thinking, trying to figure out how the guy I'd known since age four could end up dead from carbon monoxide. Finally, I said, "I still don't believe it. Something's missing. It just doesn't work."

"Paul, I knew Don better than I know you, and I have to admit I have doubts too. When Ellie left him, I can imagine Don turning to his car as a way to alleviate his frustrations. I don't see someone servicing his car suddenly deciding on suicide. Ellie says he wasn't working on his car when she left for the airport."

I said nothing.

Chuck let me think for a minute before continuing. "Some people around town are saying she hit him over the head, closed the door, and drove away, only to come back and ask us to accompany her home and find him dead. We don't have the time of death figured close enough to tell us if he died before or after she left home. But I don't believe she did it. I saw her reaction when I discovered the body. The tears were real—not fake. I know fake when I see it. Anyway, don't tell anyone I said that. It's not for me to speculate. The chief believes it's suicide. That has to be good enough for me."

"I was hoping for a little more independent thought from my police department, Chuck."

"That's easy for you to say, but I need my pension. Leave all this to the police."

I looked down, thought for a minute or so, then got out of my chair and walked back to the table with the photos and sorted through them again. "I understand Don was working on a book. You hear anything about that?"

Chuck was still in his chair behind his desk, looking down. He hesitated a long moment. "We've heard about it. It's on his computer."

"Did you check it out?"

"Can't. It's password protected."

"So have Mrs. Norbeck open it."

"She tried. The password doesn't work."

"She say why?"

"Has no idea. Said you might be able to open it."

"Me?" I shook my head. "Sorry. I didn't even know he had a computer, much less a book he was writing, until yesterday. I understand it might have something interesting on it about your new Sin Club."

"The Societe Inter Nationale Club."

"Yeah, that's the one. Grosse Ile's piggy bank."

"We want the book, Paul. Better you turn that password over to us if you find it. That way we get a court order to confiscate the computer, and you stay alive."

"*What?*"

"Some serious interests around town don't want that computer opened. For some reason, they believe you can open it."

"That's insane."

Chuck didn't reply.

"Maybe Societe Inter Nationale has their hands in this," I said.

Chuck just looked down.

"What do you know about a tough little dude named Eric Gitano?"

Chuck looked up. "How do you know about him?"

"He was pointed out to me Tuesday night at Moorey's. Likes to think of himself as tough. Has a tattoo on his neck. A knife dripping blood."

"Don't fuck with him," Chuck said. "He's a thug from north France's coal region by way of the Bronx. Legro brought him in. He's his enforcer."

"I've seen worse in Iraq."

"He'd kill you for a dime if he thought you had the password. We believe he specializes in car bombs."

"So Legro wants that computer too."

"So we hear."

"How would he ever think I had the password?"

"Don's wife thinks you can open it. Word has a way of leaking out. You know how it is."

By now, it was clear I wasn't going to get anything more from the Grosse Ile Police Department, so I stood up, thanked Chuck for his trouble, and turned to leave.

"You'll let us know if you get the password, won't you?"

I hesitated for a moment, didn't reply, and walked out the door of his office. He didn't accompany me to the door. I headed down the long hallway and turned right at the security station and out the door to my car.

Chuck LaGrange had given me a lot to think about. As honest as the Grosse Ile police had always been, and as honest as I knew the sergeant to be, the thought began to roll around in my brain that the money Societe Inter Nationale had delivered in the form of taxes to the township for the new station house and patrol cars had influenced the decision to call it a suicide. Tamped down any mentions otherwise. If there was reference to Societe Inter Nationale in Don's book, the cops wanted that information to disappear every bit as much as Legro did. The cops believed the manuscript's real password would surface. That I'd be the one to find it. Then, one dark night, Don's computer would evaporate into thin air. Or Paul Steiger would evaporate into thin air. Maybe both.

They shouldn't worry, I thought. Don's password was as dead as Don. But it was okay for me to worry.

CHAPTER 13

I REPORT TO SARABELLA

I got back to the Norbeck home and made a quick call to Dick Reardon to see if he was available to fill me in on whatever it was he wanted to tell me. Six rings told me no one was home, so I hung up and ran upstairs to tell Sarabella what Grosse Ile's finest had had to say. I knocked lightly on her partly open bedroom door.

"Who is it?"

"It's me, Paul. I have a little progress to report."

"Come in."

The room was dim. Sarabella was sitting in one of several stuffed chairs arranged about the room, facing her huge bed with its finely carved headboard. I remembered it from when, as kids, Don and I explored it and its cubbyholes filled with books and odds and ends that were important to her. Over the bed still hung a portrait of Irwin Norbeck. It was smaller than the portrait of him that was hanging in the living room downstairs over the fireplace.

She was wrapped in a fluffy, light blue bathrobe and looked weak and gray. Her mouth hung slightly open, and her eyes wandered, their electric sparkle gone. Her head was tipped to one side and supported by the middle finger of her right hand and by the pillow behind her. The finger wandered back and forth on her temple. I thought a doctor should be here, but I didn't say anything. Bertie had said she'd taken his head off when he suggested it.

Sarabella spoke in a low voice. "How did the Grosse Ile Police Department treat you this afternoon?"

"I was very well received. Chuck LaGrange couldn't have been more open. He showed me what I expect was all the evidence they had. Photos, reports—everything, as far as I could tell."

"So, what did he say? Is it suicide?"

Avoiding eye contact, I said, "That's their opinion. He showed me all kinds of pictures of Don on the floor next to his workbench. There was oil on the floor he spilled as he collapsed after getting out of his car. From what I saw, he was sitting in his car with the motor running, waiting for the carbon monoxide to get him. Then he changed his mind. He stepped out of the car and slipped and fell. Then he tried to pick himself up by holding on to the bench but couldn't and swiped some tools and a glass of Coke off the bench as he fell again."

Sarabella looked into the distance for a minute, then returned her eyes to me. "Was the motor running when they found him?"

"Uh-huh."

Sarabella looked away again. Then, after a delay, she said, "If he'd changed his mind about killing himself, wouldn't you suppose he'd have turned off the engine?"

"You'd suppose."

"So why didn't he?" Sarabella's middle finger continued its movement about her temple.

"Maybe he was confused. He may not have known what he was doing at that point."

"But he knew enough to get out of the car."

"I suppose."

"And if he'd changed his mind, why not open the garage door with the door opener in his pocket?"

"Good point."

"Seems there may be a lot the police are ignoring," Sarabella said. "They're bound and determined to make it a suicide, aren't they?"

"That may be, but—"

"No buts about it."

"What I was going to say is that all the evidence he showed me leans way over to suicide. There was a close-up of his face, and it was pinkish red. I'm never going to forget it if I live to be a thousand. LaGrange says that's a sign of carbon monoxide poisoning."

"That all they have?"

"And Don had a big bump on the side of his head where he hit the floor when he fell out of the car. That probably stunned him long enough for the carbon monoxide to do its job."

There was a silence. I could think of nothing to add.

Then, looking across the room, Sarabella said, "Did they say anything about Don's book?"

"They said they want it."

"Are you going to let them have it?"

"It's not mine to give. It's on Don's computer. It's Ellie's now."

"Do they know that?"

"I believe they do."

"What did they say?"

"They want me to give them the password if I find it."

"Don't give it to them."

"What am I going to do if I find it?"

"You could put a hammer to the computer."

"You know that's destroying evidence. The police don't like that."

"Not if they don't find out about it."

"But you know they will."

Her eyes narrowed. "Paul, that book's got to disappear."

"I'll do what I can, but I'm not going to break any laws. Not going to happen."

"Just make it disappear." Sarabella laid her head back on the pillow and closed her eyes.

"Sarabella, let's change the subject. What was Don doing back here on Grosse Ile after working himself into a great job in New York City and getting married?"

After a delay, Sarabella opened her eyes and looked at me. "He had it made in New York City. Ellie's friends loved him. He was in what some people call high society. Powerful friends. Rich friends. They thought of Ellie as their daughter. They loved her so much. From what I surmised when I met them, they would have prevented the marriage if they hadn't approved of Don. Her friends were that close to her."

"So why move back to Grosse Ile?"

"Don started doing research on his grandfather and came across some of Grandpa Sam's archives showing how he worked his way into the automobile design business. Don was so fascinated by what he found he started writing a book about him. As he got further into it, he ran across some sketches of new ideas Sam had drawn up for improving automotive transmissions that he hadn't gotten around to exploiting before he died. Don took these ideas, along with some new ideas of his own, to Ellie's friends in New York and convinced them to throw in some money."

I grinned. "Don was always a fast-talker."

"Don said it was a little dicey approaching these people because some of them get very ouchy if the cash flow isn't positive. He thought Ellie would keep them off his back if things went south."

"Okay, but why move back here?"

"Don moved back here to get closer to Detroit automotive interests. They moved into a little house here on Grosse Ile to keep expenses low. As he got deeper into his project, sure enough, he found he would need more funds than he originally thought. Good old Mom bailed him out."

"Where does Dickie Reardon fit into all this? Don never much liked the guy. None of us do."

"He tied in with Dick Reardon for access to machine shop facilities. As you can guess, that turned out to be a mistake—a big mistake. What an ass that guy turned out to be. Even started making moves on Ellie."

Sarabella's gaze drifted to the window. I began to think she wanted me to leave, but then she continued in the same low voice.

"Anyway, the project was moving forward, and Don seemed optimistic about it. Then this happened."

"That's quite a story. Now Reardon thinks he's going to continue on with it."

"That ass hasn't a prayer. He better hope Don's friends in New York have developed a sense of humor about money, which they didn't have when I met them before the wedding."

I decided to change the subject again and told Sarabella about my dinner date with Susan at the Sin Club next Tuesday. She looked at me and smiled.

"Please, Sarabella. Don't read anything into it. It's just dinner."

Sarabella raised her eyebrows, smiled, and weakly shrugged. "Of course, dear boy. What else?"

Her eyes closed, but she was still smiling when I left the room. Perhaps I should have been thinking about what Sarabella meant by that last comment. But I wasn't. I was wondering when I would see Dick Reardon to finish our discussion.

CHAPTER 14

SLEEPY-TIME TALK

For years since high school, I'd put my longing for Susan in a sealed box way back in the corner of my brain and pretty much forgot it was there. I was determined it would stay there. I'd met many other women in my travels, maybe not as gorgeous but far more grown-up, more rounded in their personalities, and minus the hang-ups. Now that I'd seen what she'd become, I figured it wouldn't be a problem keeping her in that sealed box. But it was. Over the past few days, that yen for her had flamed out of its lockbox back into my life. She was back in my thoughts. Here I was, in my room next to hers, still thinking about her. Way too much. And against all logic, I was hoping she would appear again tonight.

And she did.

It was after eleven, and I was in my shorts reading a book when my door opened. I looked up and said, "What a surprise, my love. You're early. It's not even midnight."

"I wanted to get an early start before we forget where we left off." There was a twinkle in her eye as she knelt at my feet and worked her hand along the inside of my thigh, as she liked to do. I hardened, and she went down on me in a flash.

It was a long time before I got up the emotional strength to tenderly push her away. "Later. The loving's on the menu, but we have to talk first. We have to." I hoped my words would strengthen my resolve. "If we wait, I'll forget what I want to say, or else I'll be too tired to consider it at all important."

She pouted. "What do you want to talk about?"

"I just want to fill you in on my day. I didn't get into it at dinner." I knew I was being a coward by avoiding the subject I had to discuss with her sooner or later: our involvement and how it wasn't going to happen.

"Oh, your day is very important to me, dear. Please tell me everything."

"For one thing, I visited Chuck LaGrange at the station, and we had an interesting talk."

"What did he have to say?"

"They're pretty sure it was suicide."

"I know that. And it probably was."

"They had me nearly convinced too. But I have a problem with the death threats going around."

Susan frowned. "There aren't any death threats going around. Where'd you hear that?"

"From your mother. From Joan Worth. Says her boss got them when he was thinking about publishing Don's book. Says they came from a character by the name of Eric Gitano. I think you know who he is."

"Oh him. He's full of himself. Wants to be important. Why would he be throwing around death threats?"

"I have no idea why such a fine gentleman as he would do that," I said. "I saw him at Moorey's when I first arrived Tuesday night. I was there with Bill and Tom. We were just having a few, talking about how we couldn't believe Don was a suicide. They told me all about him."

Susan frowned again and looked away for a moment, then back to me. "I'll talk to Charles about that. He should keep that animal in a cage."

I didn't reply.

"Darling, he's all talk." Her hand returned to my thigh. "I know him, and I know Charles. Gitano can't do a thing without Charles's okay. Nothing. And Charles would never let him harm you or anyone."

"I guess we're having our first lovers' quarrel," I said, "because I don't believe you. Not one word."

"My love, when you get to know Charles Legro, you'll believe me."

"Any chance he knows about the book Don was writing?"

Susan thought for a few seconds. "Maybe."

"How would he know? Would Don have told him?"

"Don wouldn't have told him. He didn't tell anyone because no one other than our family would be interested in it. All Don told me was the book's title. I assumed it was just stories about the Norbeck family. It was a family memoir."

"If Gitano is throwing around threats," I said, "it means he knows about the book, and if he knows about the book, your friend Legro knows about it and told him about it. So the question is, How did Legro find out?"

"Who knows?"

"Maybe you told him. You seem to know him pretty well."

"Well, maybe I do, and maybe I did. So what?"

"And what did you say about it?"

"I told him it was all about the Norbeck family and Sam's mansion and what Societe Inter Nationale has done with it. He seemed interested. But that's all I said. What else could I tell him? I have no idea what's in the book, or even if there is a book."

"What did Don tell you about his book?"

"Nothing. Just the title."

"You told all that to Legro, and all you knew about it was the title?"

"Sure. What's the big deal?"

"What's the title?"

"*Two Bridges to Sin.*"

"Oh, for Christ's sake, Susan. You've got to be kidding."

"No, I'm not."

"Does Charles know the title?"

"Sure. I told him."

"Of course you did. Why did I ask?"

"What do you mean?"

"Really? *Two Bridges to Sin*? A title like that could put all kinds of ideas in Legro's pea brain."

Susan smiled a satisfied smile. "I think it did. He cut twenty grand off my gambling debt when I told him."

"You know what you did? You made him think it's about his club. You have no idea what's really going on over there. You only see the dining room and the casino."

"What do you mean?"

"I hear a lot of bad shit is happening in that club of his. Legro could be very, very worried about what's in the book."

"Couldn't be much. It's just another casino. There are casinos everywhere. Gambling and great food. Big deal. If anything, it could be great publicity for him if the book ever gets published."

"But not the publicity he wants."

"I know Charles. I trust him. That casino is way too big a deal for him to risk being caught doing something wrong. And besides, Charles is a good man. He's calling me a lot now, inviting me to dinner with very important out-of-town friends. Almost to the point that I wish he'd slow down."

"Why's that?"

"He's starting to get tiresome." She looked away.

"Why don't you tell him? Tell him he's getting tiresome."

"Maybe I will."

We were quiet for over a minute, avoiding eye contact. I finally asked, "Did Don ever ask you what you might know about your family that he might put in his book?"

"Never."

"Nothing?"

"Nothing. Just the title."

"He must have been asking around. Where was he getting his information? What kind of information was he looking for?"

Susan looked bored. "Honestly, darling, Don never mentioned the book to me other than the title and that he was working on it in his spare time. He said it was a big secret and that it was on his computer and all locked up. No one was going to see it until it was published, if ever, which he said wasn't certain. Anyway, he said he was the only one with the password, so what's the big deal? The password died when he died. The book's just so many ones and zeros in his computer now. So forget it."

"Your mother hasn't forgotten it."

"What are you saying?"

"She said you told her there was something bad about the family in it. Now she's spooked."

"Oh, that." She laughed. "I only told her the title and that she wouldn't like it when the book came out, and I thought she'd wet her pants. I was pissed at her when I said it—just trying to razz her."

"I think it worked."

"Boy, did it work. I was paying her back for some of the crap she's thrown at me. Maybe I evened the score."

"You mean you were screwing with her brain?"

She nodded slowly. "And it worked. She's been a lot nicer to me ever since."

"I got a hunch you have no idea what your fairy tale started."

Her hand was back on my thigh now. She smiled, looked up at me, and said, "Bedtime for Bonzo and his Bonzette."

"Let's continue our talk in the sack. Get up."

She did and slid into my side of the bed. I opened a window, turned down the light, and rolled in beside her. What happened next, I leave to your overactive imagination. One hint: there was little talk about Don's book that made any sense, or about the subject I really wanted to discuss: our involvement.

CHAPTER 15

A TWO-DAY HANGOVER

Susan was sitting at the dining room table, and Bertie was standing at the buffet preparing a breakfast tray when I came downstairs the next morning. He pointed to it, smiled, and said, "It's for Mother's hangover."

A hangover? Really? Two days? I'd never had a two-day hangover in my life—not that I could remember anyway. I'd come close a couple of times. And I'd never heard, in all the rumors one hears in all the years growing up in a small community like Grosse Ile, that Sarabella was a boozer. Oh sure, there were plenty of heavy drinkers on Grosse Ile, and we all heard the rumors of their misadventures, but never Sarabella. Sarabella was at the very top of the Grosse Ile society food chain. She set the rules for social decorum others were to follow. She was our local gold standard, etiquette-wise, and anyone falling short of her standards got severely talked about at the bridge tables and country club luncheons in the days to follow.

But, let's face it, it was her Wednesday-night farewell to Don, a once-in-a-lifetime command performance. Now she was in the middle of a gargantuan hangover and didn't have the party history we more experienced guzzlers fell back on for support. She'd earned the pain.

Susan warmed to my arrival and motioned for me to sit next to her. I invented an excuse to sit across the table from her to avoid her hand scrabble.

She frowned. "Good morning, my dear. Sleep well?" As if to forgive my affront, she reached for the pitcher of orange juice, poured a glass, and pushed it across the table toward me. "Have you any plans today for your investigation?"

"I called Ellie. I'm going to stop by after breakfast. I'm curious to hear her side of the story. Must have been a hell of a shock to find Don there on the floor."

"I asked her about it a couple of days ago," Bertie said, "and she wouldn't say a word. Said she was trying to get it out of her mind. Maybe you'll have better luck."

Bertie turned and looked for a napkin, found one, refolded it, and placed it carefully on the tray for his mother. Then he lifted the tray and, without saying anything more, stepped out of the room.

"I must say, he is good to his mother," Susan said after he was out of hearing range. "Not like him to be so affectionate. Mattie could just as easily do all that."

"He's worried about Sarabella," I said. "I am too. Bertie said it's necessary to keep her from being pissy."

"Yeah, but his intense care for Mom's every whim is over the top. And at the same time, he keeps saying she's planning to take him out of her will. How obvious can you get? He's sucking up to her. It's sickening."

Mattie walked in with a plate of fried eggs, home fries, and toast. "Good morning, Paul. Hope you slept well. I know how you like your eggs. Call if you need a refill." She placed them in front of me, glanced at Susan to see if she needed anything, said nothing more, and returned to the kitchen. How much she had heard of our conversation I had no idea, but I assumed she heard it all. I had no problem with that. I wondered if Susan did.

I took a bite of toast. "Pass the marmalade. So what's wrong with trying to be on her good side? Makes sense to want a few bucks from her when she goes."

She rolled her eyes and laughed. "Can you believe he thinks she wants to frame him for Don's death? He actually believes that. He's doing her breakfast because he's scared she wants to put him in jail. That's wild."

"Susan," I said, "get over it. He's very worried about her. He's her only son now. He's a very intelligent guy, and he's worried sick she may not recover. You should be too. You could make her breakfast too. Or maybe her lunch."

"That'll be the day," Susan said with a derisive chuckle. "Sure I'm worried, but I'm also aware that making her breakfast every morning would not change her opinion of me one iota. That's not the way to do it. What she wants from me is for you and me to get back together again."

"We were never *together*, and it's not going to happen now. We both know that last night and the night before were pure unadulterated *lust* with a capital F. Don't get me wrong. I'm not complaining. It was fun."

"It was good for me too, Paul. But we did have something going back in high school. I know you haven't forgotten, and I'm still in love with you."

"I think you've got it backward. I was the one who fell. You were just playing with me. The first time George Herrin looked at you, I was skin rash. You wanted to have the school champion quarterback in your hip pocket, and you got him. You cut my heart out when you did that, and I'll never forget … ever. And today, he's a big nothing. Never even played in college. Couldn't even get an athletic scholarship. Talk about dumb."

"Oh, come on now. That was only puppy love back then, and you know it."

"Not for me. It was the real thing, and it's not going to happen again. You should've gotten the message when you tried to get back with me after your hero graduated and dropped you like an out-of-bounds football. I'll bet you never saw him again."

"Maybe not, but I still had feelings for you. I tried to explain all that to you then. I always think about you. Ever since school. The whole time you were in Iraq."

"Come on, you've been too busy with every man who walks by to think of me. I just happen to be available now. And close by."

"We can do it again, Paul."

"Not going to happen. I'm not in the market for a wife. I got no problem with a little fun and games, but don't look for permanent. Not going to happen."

"Someday it will. You'll come around someday when you decide it's time to hitch up. I know that. And when you do, you won't find a better deal anywhere. You'd be a perfect fit in our family. Mother loves you. Bertie does too. I notice he showed you his computer room. He wouldn't do that if he didn't like you. He won't let me near it. Mattie and Mother can't go near it."

"He had something he wanted me to see, that's all."

"It's more than that. If he didn't like you, you wouldn't have gotten near that room."

I thought for a minute. "He probably does like me, but it won't affect you and me."

She didn't say anything more. I finished my second cup of coffee in silence and left the room.

CHAPTER 16

ELLIE NORBECK

Ellie Norbeck's home was a two-story white clapboard design on a corner lot. I guessed it had four bedrooms and enough bathrooms to go around. An attached two-car garage faced left at the end of a short driveway leading in from the side street. The front yard was sprinkled with low bushes and grass. Easy for Don to manage.

The Reardons lived next door to the right in a home of similar size but with more trees in the front yard and sizable bushes separating the two homes. It was a tidy, middle-class neighborhood.

I parked at the curb and walked up the sidewalk to Ellie's front door, feeling uncomfortable. The door opened, and there was Ellie, dressed in dark blue slacks and a loose-fitting, white cotton pullover. She had a natural magnetism even in everyday clothes and immediately put me at ease. I could understand how a narcissist like Dickie Reardon could believe she was attracted to him. I was relieved to note that the fear I'd detected in her eyes on Wednesday was gone. She appeared to be pretty well over the initial shock of losing Don. Time heals.

She led me to the living room and motioned me to a comfortable chair. After the usual pleasantries and without offering me a drink, she got right to the point.

"Paul, Don did not do this to himself. He was not depressed. Someone murdered him. I know it."

"How can you be so sure? You weren't there when it happened, were you?"

"No, of course not."

"Then why?"

"Let me tell you." She looked away for a long moment, then back to me. "You probably know he had a temper."

"I knew that."

"You've probably heard Don and I had serious arguments from time to time."

"I'd heard."

"Sometimes to the point I would leave him and go home to let him cool down."

"Okay."

"But we always made up. None of it was permanent. I loved him, and he loved me. That day, we had a humdinger of an argument, and I packed a small bag and headed to the airport to fly to New York."

"I'd heard."

"I was really upset. Part of me was hoping Don would apologize and talk me out of going, but he didn't. He let me go."

"So, why didn't you go?"

"I went to Detroit Metro, bought the ticket, got all the way through security, sat down, and waited. But the airline announced a long delay. I waited for a while, but then they announced more delay. I wouldn't have gotten into New York until three in the morning. So I gave up, canceled the ticket, and headed back home."

"I hear you stopped at the police station on the way back and asked for an escort home. What was that all about?"

"I was afraid Don was still steaming mad and would get violent."

"Violent? Really? You just said he would never hit you."

"I know. But he was so angry when I left. So I stopped off at our police station, found Chuck LaGrange there, and asked him to follow me home. He was a doll. He understood and came home with me. I was hoping he could pound some sense into Don's head. Then he found Don in the garage."

"So I understand."

"I was horrified when I saw Don lying there."

"I imagine you were."

"I've seen dead bodies before but not of anyone I loved." She drew a breath and released it in a long sigh. "Look, Paul, I loved Don. We were devoted to each other. I would never have looked at another man."

"So what set him off?"

"Jealousy. Sometimes when he saw me talking to other men, his temper got in the way."

"I can't believe Don would ever hit you."

"I know. He just had a jealous streak he couldn't control. That's all it was. It got him in trouble more than once and sometimes left him on the outs with good friends and people he worked with."

"I've seen it."

"Sometimes I think that temper runs in the family."

"You may be right."

"He's not the only one in that family with a temper. I hear old Sam had a temper. And Sarabella can get that way sometimes."

I smiled. "We all saw it in her the other night at her party. And there're some wild stories about Sam. Some of them actually true."

Ellie thought for a minute. "You may not know this. Don and Dick Reardon had a fight the night before Don died. It was the final straw."

"What was it about?"

"Who the hell knows? Right out on our front lawn."

"Really?"

"Dick nearly beat the shit out of him. He could do it too. He was much bigger. I had to go out and break it up before Dick killed him."

"Do the police know about that fight?"

"Probably not. I don't know who would've told them. Not sure it would make any difference anyway. They want it to be suicide, so it'll be suicide."

"LaGrange mentioned bruises on Don's body. He didn't know what they were from."

Ellie didn't say anything more, and I waited a minute to think how I was going to phrase my next question. I didn't want to say what I was going to say, but I had to. "I don't know if you've heard, but there's word going around in some circles that you didn't leave home. That you hit Don over the head and closed the garage door."

"That's pure drivel."

"You have to believe me. I don't buy any of that, but it's being whispered. You know how people are."

"I know how people are."

"They're saying you stayed home, and when Don was dead, you went to the police to get them to come over so they would find the body."

"Ridiculous. Utterly ridiculous!"

"We both know that," I said, "but that's what's going around."

"Pure crap. I can prove it. I can prove where I was when Don died. I have a canceled airline ticket time stamped at the time Don died. And I'm sure there's a record of those plane delays."

I didn't say anything for a long moment. I was almost out of questions. "What about some book Don was writing? Sarabella heard about it, and she's wild. She seems to think there might be something in it that got people pissed off at Don. She thinks it might be the reason he was killed."

"Oh, that. Don showed me an early draft. It's just silly fiction. Nothing more."

"Oh, I think there's more to it than that. Sarabella is nervous about it. The police are nervous about it."

"I think it's the title. The title might have made some people nervous. Okay?"

I shook my head.

"But there's nothing to it. Besides, Don set up a password to protect his computer and his external drive. Then he gave me the wrong one."

"That doesn't make sense."

"I know. I tried it. It won't open his computer."

"So where's the right one?"

"I have no idea. He said if I had trouble with it, you could open it. But you can't. No one can. The thing won't open, period. And that password died with Don. The computer is worthless now. Just sitting in his office. Dead."

"I hope you're right."

Ellie nodded. "I am right. Don thought he was a budding author. What I saw was amateurish. He had a long way to go. He used the book mostly to kill time. It was just a hobby."

I hesitated. "I don't know if you knew, but he showed an early draft of it to a gal he knew from way back who works for a publishing company in Detroit. Don must have thought he had something there because he wanted the company to publish it."

Was that a flash of anger in Ellie's eyes?

"You're talking about Joan Worth. Don had an occasional dream of being a famous author, but he got over it soon enough. I think Joan may have talked him out of his idea of finishing the manuscript. She probably saw there was nothing there."

I wasn't getting anywhere. "Ellie, can you show me the garage?"

"Oh, sure. Of course. Follow me."

The path to the garage was through the kitchen to the pantry. She opened a door and stepped down one step to the garage floor. I followed. The small workbench stood just to the right. Her car was on the far side of the garage. Don's old collector car, a white 1964 Ford Galaxie convertible with its black canvas top, had been backed in unusually close to the wall. Its hood was still up. The oil I'd seen in the police photos was still on the floor.

"Why so close?" I asked.

"Don's car was a pain. He agreed to keep it close to the wall so as to give me lots of room for our other car."

I walked around his car. Then I turned back, opened the driver-side door, and, with some effort, wedged in and closed the door. I sat there a minute or so, trying to put myself in Don's thoughts. Finally, I noted the key still in the ignition, touched it to simulate him turning it off, then remembered he had not turned it off. I opened the door, squeezed out, closed the door, and walked past the garage door opener on the wall and the workbench with its spilled oil and tools just as Don had left them.

Then I looked at Ellie. "He didn't commit suicide."

"The cops say he did."

"Who the hell would believe he opened the door and fell on his head? It takes a major effort to wedge out that door. If he was semiconscious, he would've been stuck there. If he'd committed suicide, that's where they'd have found him."

We stood there looking around the garage for a long time, not saying anything.

Finally, Ellie met my eyes and said in a low voice, "I know who did this, Paul. I know who killed Don."

"You *know*?"

After a delay, she said, "And the problem is going to be handled."

"So, go to the police."

"Not that easy."

"Sure it is."

"There's a lot you don't understand. Just trust me. No need for you to look into it. You can go back to Akron."

"Bertie told me the same thing, but there are people—Sarabella's one—I'm one—who think the police are bought and paid for by the Sin Club, and it's why they're calling it suicide. I don't call that handling the problem. That's sweeping it under the rug."

"Go home, Paul. It's not going to be swept under the rug."

She refused to say more, and I finally gave up and left.

Our discussion had been an emotional experience for me. I seldom met women like her. And now there was a little man way in the back of my brain telling me I had met her before, and my answer to this little man was that that was probably what every man who met her thought. I had little experience with women of that caliber. They seldom entered my world. At least not on purpose.

As I walked to my car, I realized it had not been a professional interrogation. I thought of questions that had not been asked and questions she had dodged. Why was Don so sure I could open his computer? Why was she sure I couldn't? How did she know the time of Don's death if she was at Detroit Metro getting her airline ticket when it happened? She'd been gone for hours. How could she be so certain it was murder? Was it because she did it? And what did she mean when she said the problem would be handled? That was the word she used—*handled*.

I wasn't going home to Akron quite yet. I needed to bounce some ideas off other less-involved heads. Time for a meeting at Moorey's.

CHAPTER 17

FRIDAY AT MOOREY'S

I called Tom, Bill, and Joan and told them I had murder theories that were beginning to scramble my brain, and I needed to get balance and logic from people who lived here on Grosse Ile. They didn't object, as long as the first round was on me.

Moorey's was jumping when I got there. I mean *really* jumping. Fridays were never slow, and tonight was no exception. It was loud, and I was glad because the gang and I had a lot to discuss, and as long as we kept our voices low, I didn't think we would be heard.

Tom and Bill were there ahead of me, and Joan's car came into the parking lot behind me. I waited for her, and we walked in together.

I waved to Jake with two fingers raised as I walked past. He smiled, waved back, and reached for the Beefeater and two glasses. By the time Joan sat down next to me and settled in, a waiter was on his way over to the booth with our martinis.

After I'd tasted mine, I said, "Boys and girls, I have news."

"Good or bad?" Bill asked.

"Interesting."

"How interesting?" Joan asked.

"Don was murdered. Guaranteed."

"How do you figure?" Tom asked.

"Too many loose ends. All kinds of people could have done it, and no way would Don have done it."

"Who did it?" Joan asked.

I told them what I knew about Sarabella's kids. "One of them could have done it."

"Who else?" Tom asked.

"Well, there's Dickie Reardon. He lives next door to Don. I happen to know Reardon was home that afternoon cutting his lawn. They had a fight the night before. He could've gone over to continue the fight with Don and it went too far."

"That's a big *could've*," Tom broke in.

"And now he's telling me he knows who did it," I continued. "Maybe to take the blame off himself."

"Who's he saying did it?" Tom asked.

I offered a humorless smile. "He wouldn't give the name."

"Of course," Bill said. "That puts him up there ahead of Bertie, to my way of thinking. Anyone else?"

"Charles Legro."

Tom shook his head. "Sorry, Paul. I think he's above it all. He has a gold mine to run. That place of his has a license to print money. Don would be small potatoes. Legro couldn't care less about Don's little problems."

"Au contraire, mon ami," I said. "Susan has him thinking Don was about to out him with his book. She told Legro the title of Don's book, and he about shit."

"What's the title?" Tom asked.

"*Two Bridges to Sin*," Joan said.

"That's it," I said. "Can you believe it? With a title like that, Legro could imagine anything's in the book. Susan says Legro was really shook. Took twenty thousand dollars off her tab just for telling him the title. He could easily have told Gitano to do it."

Joan leaned back in her chair, took a sip from her martini, and looked at me. "Does Legro have the computer?"

"No. Ellie says it's sitting in Don's office."

"Then Legro didn't do it." Joan looked around at each of us. "Face it, guys. If Legro's that hyper about Don's book, no way would he have ordered Don killed without Don's computer in his hot little hands. He'd know the cops would confiscate it in a New York minute when they found Don's body. Or else Ellie would have it."

"So, who?" Bill asked. "Anyone?"

"Ellie Norbeck," I said.

"No way," Bill and Joan said in unison.

"Why would she do that?" Tom asked.

"Maybe she believes there are some secrets in Don's book she wants hidden. Nobody knows much about what she did in New York before Don met her. No one talks about it."

"If there's something there, I can't believe Don would spill it in a book," Tom said, shaking his head. "It doesn't make sense."

"They argued all the time," I said.

"Sure they argued," Tom said, "but they always made up. I guarantee you she wasn't fooling around. She loved him. I know that." He finished off his martini and motioned to a waiter for another.

"But if she thought the marriage was failing," I said, "one-third of the Norbeck fortune is certainly plenty of motive to kill for."

"Sorry," Tom said. "I don't buy it."

"Husbands have been killed for far less than what she's going to collect. Especially if she thought she could get away with it. And the police think it's suicide, which means maybe she will."

"She would not kill Don," Bill said, "unless she knew—*knew*—there was something in his book about those New York friends of hers. And all she's seen of the book is what Don showed her. Sorry, Paul. She's innocent. Look somewhere else."

The others nodded agreement.

"I can't believe any of the above did it," Joan said. "None of them have the password, so none of them would have taken such a huge gamble—killing him—without actually knowing what was in the book and having possession of the computer. No one could risk it. I think there's still a chance Don did it. We just haven't found the reason why."

"Sorry, guys," I said. "I will not believe Don did it. I'm going to keep digging."

"Nothing wrong with that," Tom said.

"I can't believe you disagree with my impeccable logic." I gulped down the last of my drink and stood up to leave.

"Sit down, Sherlock," Bill said. "I just ordered another round on your tab."

It was a round I didn't need, but I did as I was told. And besides, it would help when I returned to my room next to Sarabella Norbeck's horny daughter.

I was about to further chastise my jury of three for weak logic when a guy twisted around from the booth next to us and interrupted my train of thought. He looked at Joan and said, "Excuse me, but I couldn't help overhearing what you said about the Norbeck computer."

It was Eric Gitano. His face was a triangle ending in a pointed jaw. The nose was a stone chisel. His horizontal mouth with its dull red lips could have been cut into his face with a crude knife. Barely visible on his neck above the collar of his black golf shirt was the tattoo of a small knife dripping red blood.

Joan said, "Who asked you, Eric?"

"I just thought I'd mention how finding that computer password might not be in your best interest."

"Why's that?"

"Tell your new friend here about the death threats."

"How would you know about death threats?" Joan asked.

Eric Gitano was standing now, looking down at us. "Oh, I don't know—word gets around." He smiled with just his lips, turned his head, and looked into my eyes for a long moment. There was no humor in his smile. "Who's this?"

I edged out of our booth, stood up, turned, and looked down on him. He was short and stubby and powerfully built.

"I'd be happy to tell you who I am," I said, poking him hard in the chest—one—two—three times. "I'm the worst enemy anyone who might want to threaten my friends here could possibly have. Who're *you*—friend?" I poked him again.

"Push me in the chest one more time, I kill you," he said. His smile was gone.

Joan quickly broke in. "Paul, you're looking at a very important man. He's Eric Gitano. He works at Societe Inter Nationale. Maintains law and order there for Mr. Legro."

"Really? Doesn't look big enough for the job." I poked him again in the chest.

This time, Eric Gitano smiled. "Don't do that, Mr. Steiger. Mr. Legro tells me you spent some time in Iraq. Know all about IEDs. You should know we have them here too. More sophisticated. Can appear under your car anytime, day or night."

My Iraqi gut burn had been trying to get out of its box the past several days, and now it did. The visual, of close friends in the vehicle ahead of me enveloped in a sheet of fire, returned. I could smell it. My PTSD was back. I hoped it didn't show.

Joan glared at Gitano. "Eric, get lost. We were just having a quiet evening until you got here. Go on. Take off. Get outta here, or I'll call Jake."

A weak smile returned to Eric Gitano's lips and quickly disappeared. "I didn't mean any harm," he said, eyebrow raised, his hands up in front of him. "Just words of advice."

"Okay, so now goodbye." Joan was shaking.

Eric Gitano backed away, then turned and left. I sat back down, half smiling in disbelief.

"He's an animal, Paul. Don't fuck with him," Tom said. He was the second guy to say that to me in the past couple of days.

CHAPTER 18

HIGH FINANCE

To my welcome surprise, Susan's door was open and her room was empty when I got back to the house. It was late, and I jumped in bed and fell into a two-martini sleep. Obviously, I had not performed to her expectations last night, and she was finding her favorite form of exercise elsewhere.

But I was quite wrong, as I discovered when she came in the room very much later, turned on the overhead light, jumped on me, and said, "Gotta have light this time, big boy. I want to see what's happening."

It was a minute or so before I could pull my brain together and focus. All she had on was perfume. My watch said it was after four in the morning.

I said, "Turn off the goddamn light, *dear*. I'll explain things to you in the dark as we go along."

"Don't mess with me, Paul. I'm in a very pissed-off mood. Don was going to get all Mom's money and leave Bertie and me without a fucking dime. I've been thinking about it all day. Now I got it all figured out. He could do it. He had Mom's power of attorney. He was executor of her estate. I just found out from Charles how it works."

"Charles who?"

"Charles *Legro*, goddamn it! Who the hell else around here is named Charles?"

"How would I know? I've been gone three years, and besides, who made Charles an expert on the Norbeck estate?"

"He knows a hell of a lot more than you ever will. I had dinner with him tonight at his club, and he 'splained it all to me."

"I thought the place was closed."

"It is. We ate in the kitchen. He made dinner."

"Sounds intimate."

"It wasn't. It was all business."

"Yeah, right. Till four in the morning."

"He told me what a power of attorney is and told me Mom had given Don power over her estate."

"So what? Even if Don had power of attorney, he couldn't do anything with her money without her approval."

"You know she's said many times she was going to disinherit us. Many times. And you know she means it."

"Sorry, but I don't know she means it. Just the opposite. She was just trying to light a fire under your asses. She wants you to amount to something. That's all."

"Without my share of that money, I would die. I would have to marry money to amount to anything, and the guys out there with money are all losers. Besides, I want to marry you, and you haven't got any."

"Oh, shit."

"Oh, darling, I didn't mean it that way."

"Sure you did."

"I just meant that with my money, our life would be so fabulous. You could take me places I've never even heard of, do things that you could never afford on your salary. That's what I meant."

"I know what you meant. Without your money, I'm a loser."

"That's *not* what I meant, and you know it."

"Forget it. I couldn't care less what it meant. Change the subject."

"Okay. Let's see." She thought for a minute, then looked very serious. "Okay, tell me how you're making out on who killed Don. Any progress?"

I said no. But it was a lie. I'd just added another person to my list of suspects. Her.

She sat there for a minute, staring at the far wall, looking as if she was trying to think of an intelligent question. Finally, she looked back down at me, smiled a naughty smile, and quietly said, "Let's get down to business."

Tired as I was, we did just that.

CHAPTER 19

SAMUEL IRWIN NORBECK

S usan was still in her room when I got down for breakfast, and Bertie was there for a breakfast of his own, having just returned from taking a breakfast tray up to Sarabella. All he said was, "Mother's better."

I always wished I'd known Don Norbeck's grandfather. Everyone said Samuel Irwin Norbeck was a crusty, eccentric, and very successful auto pioneer from the 1920s until retirement in 1954. Some said he patented other people's ideas and profited hugely from them. As a result, Detroit's elite hated him and refused him membership in their fancy clubs. One club made the mistake of letting him join, and within a year, they ejected him for starting a fight late one night involving a dozen members that continued down four flights of stairs to the front door.

Sam Norbeck had many enemies and received many death threats, so he built a mansion on the island of Grosse Ile, thinking it was safer there for his wife, Marion, and only son, Irwin. He located the mansion on the shore facing Canada and specified it to be of heavy Teutonic architecture fortified with gunports and a large gun arsenal. The land inside the high wall surrounding the house was clear of growth to eliminate cover for enemies approaching from land or water. Each room had hidden panels that opened to passageways leading to a tunnel for escape so attackers couldn't trap him. Two boat wells housed high-powered boats he said he wanted to experiment with, but people all knew the boats were there to allow for escape by water.

They finally got to him in 1960—a knife in the back. In his home. People believed Sam couldn't get to a safe room no one's ever found, that his murder was a mystery that would never be solved. He was hated by a lot of rich people, and, let's face it, professional killers are a dime a dozen.

But there was a lot more about him I didn't know. I walked over to a tray of French toast and bacon Mattie had prepared for us, helped myself, and said to Bertie, "Your grandfather was a hell of a guy to accomplish what he did."

"He was indeed. You have no idea how his mind worked."

"Do you know how his mind worked? He died before you were born."

"I can tell you this: he was fascinated with machinery from an early age, probably when his family lived on a farm and he operated the early farm machinery—tractors, combines. You know. He loved to take them apart and put them back together better than before."

"What was Sam like? As a person, I mean."

"If you ever ask Mother, she'll tell you Sam was an asshole. For some reason, she hated his guts."

"How could she hate him that much? She never met him, did she? She was only fourteen when he was murdered."

"True." Bertie poured himself a second cup of coffee.

"I heard he was liked in some quarters," I said. "Wasn't there anything about him you could like?"

"Not as far as I ever heard Mother say. She always said he was a mean drunk. Said the world was better off with him dead. She said when he drank, he got obnoxious, and people had to walk away from him. He'd get in fights. You've heard those stories."

"He obviously was bright," I said. "He had some incredible ideas, and he clearly made them pay off. Someone must have liked him for him to accomplish so much. I hear Marion was a nice person."

"Mom said she was a sweet lady. Said she never had much to say but was certainly an improvement over Grandpa. Wondered how she stood Sam all those years."

"Sounds like your dad took more after her than his father."

"Mom told us Dad was a wonderful man, wished us kids had known him, said he would've been a fine influence on us. She said many times Susan and I needed a father like him when we were growing up, which was probably true."

"Probably got his brains from Sam," I said.

Bertie didn't reply to this, and I decided we didn't need to get any deeper into a study of Irwin's character, or we would enter the verboten neighborhood of why he committed suicide.

"What did Sam do to earn all his money if he was such an asshole? You said you helped Don study up on him."

"First of all, he wasn't an asshole. After high school, he went to the University of Michigan and ended up with a job in an early auto company no one's heard of today. They put him to work on transmission design. At the time, transmissions were way too big, and the company wanted them to be smaller. They just couldn't figure out how to do it back then. So this got Sam involved in gear tooth design, which at the time was settled technology. But Sam got good at it, and one day he got an idea. He went to his boss with it and got shot down."

"Why?"

"He suggested violating orthodoxy. You just didn't do that back then."

"What had he suggested?"

"He wanted to change the shape of the gear tooth."

"So?"

"Let me give you a little history."

"Do it."

"In the late nineteenth century, machine designers had perfected a gear tooth contour they called 'involute.' What that tooth contour achieved was pure rolling contact between gear tooth surfaces, resulting in a huge increase in gear life, quiet operation, and reduced cost to produce. Previous gear contours caused a rubbing action between tooth surfaces. This greatly limited gear life and made them noisy."

"If the new design was so good, why change?"

"There was one drawback to the classic involute gear tooth design. It only worked for certain very specific distances between the gear shafts. This caused the automotive transmission case to be very large, which meant automobile designers had to raise the frame of the car to minimize the hump in the floor intruding on the passengers' feet. Passengers complained of difficulty getting into and out of cars back then, especially women in their long, ruffled skirts."

I was fascinated. I sipped my coffee.

"Sam went to his boss with his idea. If he were to significantly alter the classic involute gear tooth contour, he could reduce gear shaft distances. This would shrink the size of the transmission. His boss was horrified. Gear manufacturers had worked out the involute tooth contour geometry the previous century, and it was sacrosanct. Gear manufacturers and auto companies had invested millions of dollars in huge involute gear-cutting machines and couldn't imagine throwing them all out and investing in new machines. Besides, as far as they were concerned, the complaints of a few customers over the height of the car were nothing compared to the complaints they would receive if the life of the gears collapsed and required constant transmission replacements."

Mattie entered the dining room silently and placed more French toast in front of me.

I thanked her with a smile. "Keep going, Bertie."

"Everyone Sam talked to thought his idea was stupid and told him so. His boss said the idea was ridiculous, that the gears would be weak and noisy. He threw him out of the office. No one ever accused Sam of being diplomatic, and when he persisted, they fired him."

"So how did Sam get around the problem?"

"He discovered there was no problem."

"No problem?"

"Nope. Sam found data showing that few cars put more than fifty hours on the first and second gears in their lifetime. So why use classic involute gear teeth? By going to special gear teeth, which he would design, the distance between gear shafts is less, and the gear case is smaller. Sure, it would be noisy in first and second, but the teeth would survive because they would never see fifty hours of use. The transmission was silent in third gear because there was no gear tooth involvement in third gear."

I swallowed a bite of French toast and said, "Didn't Sam point this out to his superiors?"

"Sure, but they didn't buy his fifty-hour number. They scoffed at his ideas, said over and over again these gear teeth would be too fragile and too noisy. Ultimately, they were too afraid to take a chance Sam might be wrong."

"So?"

"By now, Sam was a gear-design wizard without a job and fully confident he could design a better transmission."

"So what did he do?"

"He started his own gear company, patenting his very special gear tooth contours. Sam struggled at first and became very bitter when certain auto companies tried to hinder his work. But he persevered, working night and day at home to pioneer and patent the formulae, graphs, and tooth profiles that are used in modern automotive gear systems to this day, including today's automatic transmissions."

"Impressive," I said, and meant it.

"The rest is history. He designed a compact three-speed automotive transmission, far smaller than what was in use at the time, and a couple of auto companies tested it out."

"And it worked?"

"It worked like a charm." Bertie stopped long enough to spread marmalade on a piece of toast. "As a result of their tests, they contracted Sam for a year's supply."

"If they hated Sam, why not make their own transmissions?"

"They had to use Sam. Sam had patents by now, so he had exclusive rights to supply them all the downsized transmissions they could use. In one year, a number of other car companies saw what he had invented and ponied up. By now, Sam had no problem getting funds to expand, going public and selling stock, and getting loans from the banks."

"This is how he got rich," I said.

"His bank account exploded. Few people have ever heard of his company because he sold only to car companies, and besides, who's interested in gear tooth design? People who like cars think of style, colors, acceleration, top speed—not what's under the hood, other than the engine."

"So Sam was a hero." I dribbled syrup on my last piece of French toast and took a bite.

"Yes and no," Bertie said. "Sam had produced a lot of transmissions, put a lot of money in the bank, but at the same time made a lot of enemies in the car business doing it. To get there, he'd been very ruthless, and his efforts eventually put several big gear companies out of business and left their owners penniless."

"Couldn't those companies have bought licenses to produce his gears?"

"Yeah, if he'd let them. But he didn't. He refused them access to his patents."

"Why?"

"He was very bitter at the way they had scoffed at him when he first proposed his ideas and then put up roadblocks when he tried to start his company. So companies went belly-up. A lot of people ended up on the street, including some very powerful people. Some very bad people. People with ties to the Detroit gangs. Sam started getting threats."

"That's why he built his mansion on Grosse Ile?"

"Yeah."

"And dug that tunnel?"

"Yeah. It was his escape tunnel that he would use if enemies attacked him in his mansion. It extended over two hundred yards west into a field across the road." Bertie was on a roll now. "Sam went to extreme expense building defenses into that mansion. The place had a safe room, as you know, stacked with enough supplies for weeks, disguised so well no one ever found it."

"What about his boats? He liked to experiment with high-powered boats, didn't he?"

"They were really there so he could escape by water if they came after him by land."

"He lived in fear, didn't he?"

"In spades," Bertie said. "Rightly so, as it turned out."

"Did he figure out those defenses all by himself?"

"No. He patterned them after a smaller house over on the other side of Grosse Ile. A high official of the Ford Motor Company built it several years earlier. Henry Ford's buddy."

"Who was that?"

"Harry Bennett. He had enemies too—like Sam. But they never got to him. He was too smart. He died of old age."

CHAPTER 20

SARABELLA AGAIN

Sarabella's eyes were closed when I walked into her bedroom after lunch. She looked like she'd shit and missed and got shit at and hit. Old army expression.

She heard me walk in and said weakly, "Is that you, Mattie?" Then her eyes opened briefly. "Oh, it's you. What do you want?"

Pillows propped her up in her huge bed. In better days, she referred to it as her workbench—where she and Irwin made babies. Her head lay partially tipped on the pillow behind her, and her mouth was curved down. Her skin had no color, and her hair was unkempt.

"I have an update for you. I can put it off if you'd rather."

"No. No. Come on in. Sit."

"How are you feeling? Any better at all?"

"The vertigo is still with me, the headache never ceases, and I can't eat. Nausea. Bertie took my blood pressure and says it's high. Tells me I should stop drinking." Her eyes were closed again.

"You should be in a hospital. Why hasn't a doctor been here?"

"I don't want one, and besides, Bertie says they don't make house calls. Anyway, I don't feel that bad. Another day in bed, and I should be better."

"Sarabella, I've been talking to people and checking around. It wasn't suicide."

"That's what I've been saying."

"I told you I talked to Chuck LaGrange."

"I don't trust those bastards as far as I can throw them."

"I told you he said the department is calling it a suicide, but the longer

I think about it, the more it sounds like maybe it was an accident. Maybe it was just a very bizarre accident."

"It was no accident," Sarabella said, lifting her head from the pillow, opening her eyes, and looking at me.

"The cops said Don always took care of the regular service for his car himself. When you check the automatic transmission oil level, the engine must be running. The transmission dipstick was on the floor. A can of transmission oil had tipped over and spilled on the floor. Don could have dropped the can, slipped on the spilled oil, fallen, and hit his head. A remote control for the garage door was in his pocket. It could have triggered the door closing when he fell."

Sarabella slowly shook her head. "That's a stretch, Paul."

"But you have to admit it's possible."

"Bullshit is what it is. What does LaGrange think?"

"I got the impression he's not completely convinced it's suicide and just couldn't come right out with his real opinion. He mentioned something about a pension he has to think about."

Sarabella's lips moved in what might have been a humorless smile. "There you go."

"When I asked about an autopsy, he shrugged his shoulders. Said the official police position is suicide, and that's what they're going with."

Sarabella slapped a hand down on her mattress. "No, no, no, Paul. It was murder, goddamn it. I'm telling you it was murder. People knew about that book he was writing and wanted him dead. They wanted the book destroyed, and he wouldn't do it." She laid her head back on the pillow, exhausted, eyes closed, the finger pressing her temple moving slowly back and forth.

I waited.

"Anyone could have killed Don," she said finally, not opening her eyes. "Easy. Visit and hit him over the head while the car engine was running."

"And then just close the garage door?"

She hesitated. "Yes. Just close the garage door." Her eyes stayed closed.

I thought about what she said.

After a long moment, Sarabella continued. "The wall switch for the garage door is next to the kitchen door. Close the door and walk away."

"Okay, maybe that's possible." I didn't want to rile Sarabella any more than I already had, but I had to get one more thing off my chest. "Well, you asked me to look into this mess, remember, and I'm willing to do it. But I'm going to be neutral and let the facts take us where they will. As to who did it, I'm like you. I can't for the world believe Susan or Bertie could do such a thing, but you have to agree your money makes for a hell of a motive in anyone's book."

"Money might be a motive for the police, but my kids loved Don, and nothing could make them kill him. Now get the hell out of here and find out who did it. You're making my headache worse. I feel like I'm rolling out of bed. Go tell Bertie to come up."

CHAPTER 21

PASSWORDITIS

When I got downstairs, I phoned Dickie Reardon to see if he had time to fill me in on his thoughts about Don's passing. The phone was busy, which meant someone was home, so I got into my Beamer and headed over. I was running out of places to look, and Reardon was close to my last hope. He'd said if it was murder, he'd seen the murderer, but knowing him, this could all be just so much hot air. I'd never believed more than 10 percent of what he told me as long as I'd known him.

The Reardons' home was similar to Don's next door but larger and set back farther from the road to give him more grass to cut in the summer and more driveway to clear of snow in the winter. No advantages there. His garage door was closed. I parked in his driveway, picked up two folded newspapers in his yard to show good intentions, and walked to the front door.

I was about to push the doorbell when Ellie rushed out of her house next door and yelled at me to come over. I dropped the newspapers and went over.

Her smile did not hide the troubled look on her face. "Come in," she said, motioning me to a cushioned chair in the living room. She didn't sit. "I need your help."

"What about?"

"Legro phoned this morning. He wants Don's computer."

I raised my eyebrows. "That's interesting. Go on."

"He sounded serious. Says he'll do anything to get it."

"You're not going to give it to him, are you?"

103

"He says he wants it to protect the good name of that club of his. Thinks Don put rubbish about it in his manuscript." Ellie let that sink in for a moment. "It's the title of his goddamned book, Paul. Don named it *Two Bridges to Sin*. When Susan told him the title, she said he went berserk. I think Legro believes the book's all about him and what's going on in that club."

"I agree. I heard the same story. I also happen to know there's some real bad shit going on over there. He has a lot to hide."

Ellie nodded. "I'm sure there is, and I'm sure he does."

"How would Don have found out about it? Everyone says he almost never went there."

Ellie looked down.

I waited a long moment. "I thought you said his book was silly fiction."

The troubled look was still there. "Maybe it's not all silly."

I looked at the floor. "Ellie, if I'm going to help you, you're going to have to tell me a little more about what's in Don's manuscript. Is there anything actually in it that could get Legro riled up?"

"I can't believe there could be. Don told me a little about what's in the book. Said it was all about Norbeck family history. Said he'd done a lot of research on Sam Norbeck and that I'd be interested in what he found out."

"That doesn't sound like anything that would shake up Legro." After a long silence, I said, "Bertie knows a lot. He could've told Don something. He says he didn't, but maybe he did."

"Don said he'd found a lot of dirt. Didn't say where he got it or who it was about."

"Ellie … maybe the answer is to put a hammer to the computer and call up Legro and tell him to come and get it."

Ellie thought about that. "Paul, I haven't offered you a coffee. I still have a little. How about a cup?" She motioned to the kitchen.

I said I'd love some, while asking myself why she hadn't already hammered that computer to pieces. I got up out of my chair, and we walked to the kitchen. There were breakfast dishes in the sink, the coffeemaker on-light still bright red. There was enough left for one cup each. I added my usual sugar, stirred it in, and we returned to the living room. Neither of us said anything important until we both reached empty cups.

Finally, I sensed she was ready to tell me something. Maybe the real reason she'd asked me over. The interlude had given her time to decide how exactly to frame her words.

She moved to the chair next to me and looked down at the floor again, her face flushed. "I haven't been exactly truthful with you, Paul. There's more to my story ... about the day Don died."

I waited a beat and said, "Okay ..."

"I didn't want you involved in this, so I didn't tell you that on the day Don died, after the police left, Eric Gitano visited me and demanded I give him Don's computer."

My eyes widened.

"He had a gun. Said if I didn't give him the computer, he'd kill me and take it. I believed him. I took him into the house and showed him the computer. It's a large desktop and very awkward to pack up and remove to a car, so I offered to give him Don's external backup drive instead."

"He was okay with that?"

"I told him it had everything on it that was on the computer because the computer automatically backs up everything anyone puts on the computer. Gitano argued, but when he saw what was involved in disconnecting the computer, carrying it to the car, and then reconnecting it and starting it up, he agreed the external drive would be enough."

"And that was that?"

"Ah ... not quite. I told him there was a complication. Don locked the computer and the external drive with a password. I wrote it down on a piece of paper, which he stuffed in his pocket. And he left with just the backup drive and the password."

"So now he knows what's on the computer."

She hesitated. "Actually, no, he doesn't."

"And that's because the password doesn't work. Right?"

"Because I'd already tried to get into the computer with that password, and it doesn't work."

"So now Legro is coming back at you for the computer. And I'm sure he wants the correct password this time."

Ellie looked scared now. "Yeah. The trouble is, Paul, I gave Gitano the password Don gave me. I didn't alter it or change it. Don wanted me to be able to get into the computer if anything happened to him. He didn't want the information he'd discovered to disappear."

"But maybe it has," I said. "If the password is the wrong one. We have no way to get into the computer."

"I know that, Paul. I know that. But Don insisted it was the correct password and said that if I had any trouble getting in, you could help."

"Me?"

"The way he said it was almost as if he expected I would have trouble with the password. He explicitly said you could figure it out. Several times."

"How the hell would he expect me to help? I didn't even know the computer existed until a few days ago. I didn't know he was writing a book."

"He kept saying you would know how to get in if I gave you the password."

I slowly shook my head. "What is it?"

"The password is *paulsteiger*. Your name. All one word."

"My name?"

"Lower case. Period. Full stop."

I could only continue to shake my head slowly. Finally, I said, "Let's go look at the brute."

We got up and headed to the computer in Don's office. It was an Apple desktop, just as Ellie had said. Their big one. It had a huge, twenty-seven-inch screen. Wires connected it to a wall socket, two printers, an audio system, and other mysterious black boxes around the table. Reason enough why Gitano didn't want to carry it to his car.

I sat down in front of it, looked it all over, and fired it up. Its screen lit up fine, but that was all it did. Nothing worked. It looked back at me and adamantly demanded Don's password before it was going to perform any of its miracles.

"This is as far as I could get," Ellie said.

I entered the password. It failed. I tried it again, this time in caps. Of course it failed. Then with only a capital *P*, the rest lowercase. Again it failed. I continued testing various combinations of alternate caps and no caps. I typed it backward. Nothing worked.

I sat back and looked at Ellie. "I'm sorry, Ellie," I said, "but that is *not* the correct password. He could have changed it without telling you. Have you looked for a piece of paper with some letters and numbers on it under desk drawers, in files in his desk, in the bedroom—all over the house?"

"All over the house. I've looked everywhere. In the house, in the car, in the safe deposit box—everywhere. You name it, I've looked."

I leaned back in Don's chair and looked up at the ceiling. Ellie was across from me. We sat in silence for what seemed like minutes. Nothing. I just sat there trying to come up with a new thought. And nothing came to me. The chair squeaked a brief squeak, a clock ticked somewhere, and I was comfortable. But that was all.

I leaned farther back and stared into deep space. Something was out there, way out there, trying to break in through the wall around my brain. I thought of a lot of things. I thought of our life growing up and then of a photo Mom had taken of two sixteen-year-old troublemakers looking for more trouble. We had the usual look Don and I presented whenever someone with a camera pointed it at us. What was it we were thinking when Mom took that photo?

Age sixteen was about the time Don liked to bug me about the spelling of my name. "Paul," he used to say, "we were taught in English class that *I* came before *E* except after *C*, so why do you spell your name Steiger? Why not Stieger?'"

He loved to bug me about it, even after we got out of school. He got a big laugh out of it.

I leaned forward and typed *paulstieger* into the computer.

We heard a distant gunshot. Then another. They sounded close. Maybe next door.

CHAPTER 22

THE REARDONS ARE HOME

We looked at the computer—it was coming to life—then at each other for maybe a minute. Finally, we got up from our chairs and walked to the front door and looked out. Nothing.

"We better check," Ellie said.

I nodded and shut down Don's computer. We walked next door, and I pushed the doorbell. I waited, then pushed it again. I could hear it ring inside. We looked at each other, waited awhile. Then I knocked hard on the door. I waited some more, then for some reason cautiously turned the doorknob and pushed lightly on the door.

It opened no more than a few inches, and there it was: a smell I'd hoped I'd left in Iraq. The familiar smell of gunpowder and death. It brought back memories I never wanted to revisit, and I wanted to close the door. But I didn't.

I opened the front door wide, and we went into the living room, looked around, and opened a couple of windows. Nothing was out of place. I looked in the kitchen. Ellie checked the dining room, then the family room. It all looked normal. I remembered reading somewhere that the authorities prefer you not to disturb a crime scene, but oh hell, I decided I had better confirm it was a crime scene before I didn't disturb it.

Upstairs, the smell intensified in the direction of a bedroom down the hallway. It was the Reardons' master bedroom. We walked into a large room dominated by a king-size bed to the right and a sixty-five-inch flat-screen TV on a table against the opposite wall. On either side were his and hers dressers on which stood an array of photo reminders of close friends important to a family with no children.

Dickie Reardon was lying beside the bed.

"That's a contact wound," Ellie said.

A black, star-shaped burn on his temple surrounded a small black hole. A gun barrel pressed tight against his head would have caused this kind of burn. Gases would get under the skin and then blast back out. Like the contact wounds I'd seen in Iraq.

Anne was lying on the floor at right angles to him and some distance back with a neat black dot on her temple surrounded by a black, round burn ring. It was a smudge. Not a contact wound but close. Maybe two or three inches. There was no blood that I could see on the carpet near them. A small-caliber pistol lay close to Anne's right hand.

The bedside table phone was on the floor and off the hook. The bed was made and had not been disturbed. A computer station was set up over to the far left of the room near a window. The printer had one piece of paper in its discharge tray.

Ellie went over to it and carefully picked it up so as not to disturb fingerprints, then held it out for me to read.

To whom it may concern

My life is over. I cannot live knowing my husband is a murderer. He killed Don Norbeck for no good reason. Tonight I killed him, and now I will kill myself. May we rest in peace. Anne Reardon

I fired up my iPhone and called 911. A voice said someone would be there shortly. Then we left the house. I backed my car out of the driveway and parked at the curb to allow a meat wagon in when it was time for the bodies to depart, then waited for the cops to arrive.

"You handle it," Ellie said. She went back to her home and closed the door.

So it seemed that my investigation was over. Case solved. Time for me to head back to Akron. Sarabella was vindicated. Don was not a suicide.

My old friend Sergeant Chuck LaGrange arrived first with an officer I didn't recognize. No flashing lights. Apparently, they weren't going to send in the first team on my say-so until LaGrange confirmed this was actually a crime scene. He walked over to my car.

I buzzed down a window and said, "The front door is open. Go on in. It'll make your day."

He did as I suggested. He soon exited, returned to his squad car, and called in help. His call produced a much faster response than mine had. Sirens, flashing lights, and lots of uniforms. I wondered if anyone was minding the store. They told me to wait in my car as they crowded into the house. I waited in my car and dozed off. It was easy. I hadn't gotten much sleep last night.

It was late afternoon when a detective tapped on my window to wake me and get what little information I had. I sat up in the seat and lowered the window.

"Sergeant LaGrange tells me you've been looking into the death of Don Norbeck. Is that correct?"

"Yes. Just a little curious."

"Why curious?"

"Why not? I'd known Don since we were kids. I couldn't imagine he could kill himself. It wasn't possible."

His arms were resting on my windowsill. "Any idea why Mr. Reardon would want to kill his neighbor?"

"No idea. I've only been in town a couple of days."

"What about Mrs. Reardon?"

"I thought Anne was depressed."

"Why do you say that?"

"Because she seemed depressed when I saw her at a recent meeting at Mrs. Norbeck's son's funeral a few days ago, as well as a lifetime of knowing her."

"So, are you satisfied now?"

"I suppose I am."

"You live in Akron. Is that correct?"

"That is correct."

"Any reason to stick around Grosse Ile?"

"Sure. I have friends here. I grew up here. Why not stick around?"

"Could be dangerous. People think you're nosing into this. Easy these days for bombs to find their way under cars. See it all the time in the newspapers. Cars like your beautiful BMW here. We wouldn't want that to happen, would we?"

"Your threat belongs in a comic book," I said.

"Oh really? You're from Grosse Ile, right?"

"Yes."

"You remember George McComb?"

"Sure."

"He was supervisor of the Grosse Ile Township for many years."

"So?"

"His car was bombed in a Detroit parking lot a couple of years ago when he got in it and tried to start it. Never found who did it."

I just looked at him.

"He opposed the sale of Mrs. Norbeck's mansion to Societe Inter Nationale. His replacement approved the sale." The officer hesitated, looked away for a few seconds, then back to me. "We have your home phone, Mr. Steiger. We'll contact you in Akron if there's anything we need from you. Have a good day."

He walked away, and I thought twice before starting my car. On the way to the Norbeck home, I wondered how Sarabella would take the Reardon deaths. And just how coincidental was this third car bomb comment in the past couple of days? Definitely time for me to head home.

CHAPTER 23

DINNERTIME ANNOUNCEMENT

Bertie helped Sarabella walk slowly in to dinner. She looked better than she had this morning when she almost couldn't raise her head off the pillow but just barely. Walking in to dinner was a big plus. Maybe she'd turned the corner. I hoped so.

As usual, she sat at the head of the table. Her head was bent, and she stared at the dinner plate in front of her. She said nothing. Bertie sat to her left, and Susan to her right. I chose to sit next to Bertie, away from Susan's exploring hands. I had serious business for them and didn't need the distraction.

We'd finished a salad in silence, and Mattie had already cleared the table when I looked around at everyone and said, "Sarabella, I have some news for you that I want you to hear from me before you hear it anywhere else."

"What is it?" Bertie asked.

"The police have confirmed Don was murdered."

Sarabella looked up. "What?" Her eyes were wide open.

"Don was murdered. You were right. The police were wrong."

They all looked at me. The room went dead quiet.

"You heard it right. Don was murdered by Dickie Reardon."

"Bullshit," Bertie said.

"And Anne killed Dickie."

Silence. They stared at me. Bertie looked like he wanted to say bullshit again.

"And then killed herself."

"What the hell are you talking about?" Bertie said.

"I found them in their home. That's where I've been all afternoon."

I went on to fill them in on what had happened—that I'd discovered their bodies in their home and called the police. I told them about Anne's note. I said that Dickie and Don had had a fight in Don's front yard the evening before Don died, and apparently Dickie had let it build up into a tornado in his mind and came back and killed him the next day while he was working on his car in his garage. "The police say it's open and shut."

Mattie had walked in to serve the main course of roast beef, mashed potatoes, and a veggie mix when I said I'd discovered the bodies. She looked as stunned as the others. "Everyone on Grosse Ile knew the Reardons," she said. "The people of Grosse Ile just don't do that sort of thing."

I let the news percolate. Sarabella looked confused and slowly shook her head and gazed off into the distance. Bertie frowned and looked down, shaking his head.

"I'm returning to Akron tomorrow," I said.

This brought Sarabella very much back to life. "You're what?"

"Sarabella, let's face it. My business here is over."

"Sorry, but there's still the matter of Don's computer and what's on it. You don't have it yet. No one knows what's on it. Don could have found anything and put it on his computer." Sarabella's voice sounded like gravel flowing slowly out of a dump truck.

"The computer is locked up, and no one has the password," I lied. "The password died with Don. It's gone. That means the computer's dead too." I wasn't about to let anyone at the table know I'd opened the computer and looked inside.

Sarabella stared at me with lifeless eyes for a long moment, her head in a slight tremor to almost match the tremor in her fingers resting on the table. Finally, she said, "It ... it's not dead, Paul. It's not dead. Experts can pry computers open. We all know that. Now I asked you to get that computer for me when you first arrived here, and I still want that goddamn computer."

I took a moment to compose a reply and present it as gently as I could. "I know you did, Sarabella, and I know you do, but that computer is legally the property of Ellie. I can only *ask* her for it. And I'm not sure she'll want to give it up. I can only try. And, besides, over the next several weeks, Bertie can try as easily as I can to get it."

Sarabella's eyes flared. "She won't give it to Bertie, and you know it, but she *will* give it to you. You were Don's best friend. You have a better reason to see what's on it."

"Like I said, I can only try."

"You *have* to get it, Paul. I don't care how. It has many Norbeck family secrets in it that are no one's business. Maybe it will tell us if Don's killer really was Reardon. I'm not that sure he did it. He had no real reason to kill Don. There are others with far better motives and stories that will never see the light of day unless we can get that computer."

"I agree there are loose ends about this whole thing. But they're *very loose* ends. Dickie and Don had business issues, we know that, and he was all over Ellie, but you usually settle those problems with your fists, which they did the night before he died. Like you, Sarabella, I can think of other people a lot more likely to have done it."

Sarabella stared at me and said nothing.

I turned to Susan. "I know you think the world of Charles Legro, but you know he's got a mean guy working for him, and maybe he thought Don was putting tales on his computer about his operation that weren't true. True or not, either way, Don could do him a lot of harm with nasty stories about the Sin Club."

Susan started to say something, but Sarabella interrupted. "All good reasons why we have to get that computer."

"On the other hand," I said, "when I talked to Ellie, she said she's seen part of what's in the book and said it was just silly fiction. That's what she called it. Silly fiction. She said Don was just fooling around with his computer. Thought of himself as a budding author."

"Don't you believe her," Sarabella said. "She doesn't want anyone getting hold of what's in it. She wants that information all for herself. As long as she has that computer, she's dangerous." Sarabella glared at me for a long, long moment and then said in a low, gravelly voice, "Paul, get that fucking computer."

If she'd had a gun in her hand, she'd have killed me there at the table without finishing the bite of roast beef on the fork she was jabbing in my direction to make her point. I stared back at her until she lowered her eyes and put that morsel of roast beef in her mouth.

The whole exchange had brought a flicker of light back into Sarabella's eyes, but I was sure it wouldn't last. She was a sick lady, and I'd only made it worse.

"Case closed," I said. "I'm heading back to Akron."

Susan frowned at me and left the room. Ten minutes later, I heard her car roar to life and zoom out of the driveway.

CHAPTER 24

LATE-NIGHT CHAT

Even before my eyes opened, the warm hand low on my stomach told me who it was. And so did the perfume. "Good morning, Susan," I said, my eyes still tightly shut. "I hope it's late morning. I needed the sleep."

"Sorry, my dear, but your evening has hardly begun." Tired didn't matter to Susan. "This is going to be your last evening on Grosse Ile, and you *will* remember it."

"Where are you, lover?" I half whispered, eyes still shut. "I can't see you in the dark."

"About to mount my stallion, sweetheart."

And so she did. It turned out to be a long ride over hill and dale. Finally, after the stallion returned to the barn, rode hard and put away wet, she rolled off me and we lay there. No talk.

It was clear to me that before I left to go home that morning, I had to make sure she understood this was not love. Lust maybe, but not love.

I also wondered why she was so late getting home this evening. Where had she been? Was she seeing someone else? But I didn't ask, and she didn't tell.

We were silent for a long time—thinking. We lay there in the dark and the stillness, our hands to ourselves.

Finally, I said, "Susan, I must say you are an exhausting person to know."

"Just *know*?"

"I think you know it's not love."

"I thought it was. It is for me."

"We both know it's passion—lust—all those lovely things, but it's not love."

"Paul, it's going to be for you. I know it will. Sometimes these things take time. We've been together in our hearts since we were kids. You're going to realize that. I know you will."

There was a long silence. I didn't know how to answer her without breaking our friendship. For me, years ago, it had been intense puppy love. Gone now for good. I could see it. Why couldn't she?

The silence continued, and I'd started to doze off when she said in a monotone, "You know that note Anne wrote is crap."

"What do you mean?"

"The note's crap."

"Why?"

"You really don't know?"

"Know what?"

"About Anne Reardon?"

"What about Anne Reardon?"

"Anne Reardon had no clue how to use a computer. She had no more idea how to type a note on a computer than speak Mandarin Chinese."

"Excuse me?"

"Anne wouldn't touch a computer."

"How do you know that?"

"She didn't even know how to turn one on. Everybody knows."

"I didn't. Not the police. They're closing the case."

"I bet they reopen it when they find out about Anne."

"If they do find out," I said, "it won't matter. They want Dickie to have done it. This ends it for them. They're glad it's over."

"Anyone on Grosse Ile who knew Anne knew she hated computers."

"So that means whoever killed Dickie didn't know," I said. "Means it was a professional hit."

"Anne would have handwritten the note if she'd done it. And on top of that, she hated guns. I doubt if they even had a gun in the house. No way she killed Dickie."

I was awake now, my eyes wide open, my head off the pillow. I could only imagine the look of triumph on Susan's face in the dark. She was tearing up my ticket outta here. I rolled over on my side and looked at the dim, featureless form beside me. "So tomorrow I look for Don's computer."

"So no you don't."

"So why not?"

"Because that computer won't help you. It's got passworditis … and besides, that's not where the answers are."

I knew she was still smiling. So I egged her on. "So, just where are the answers, my all-knowing love bug?"

"In the town of Wyandotte. Just over the river. Not ten miles from here."

"Any particular idea where in Wyandotte?"

"Go over the Grosse Ile toll bridge and go north on Biddle Avenue. Then turn left on Columbine."

"And where will that put me? Is there someone I should know on Columbine in Wyandotte?"

"There is indeed, my very sweetest sweetheart. You want to talk to a gentleman by the name of Calvin Bridges."

I thought for a few seconds. "I know Cal. A little. He's a nice guy. I saw him at the funeral. Why him?"

"You want to talk to him because he can tell you what you want to know."

"How do you know that?"

"His father was Smiley Bridges. Smiley Bridges was Sam Norbeck's chauffeur. Cal is Smiley Bridges's only son."

"Ancient history. Don died less than a week ago."

"Might explain why Mother wants Ellie's computer so badly. Don once told me Cal said he overheard his father say something bad about the Norbeck family—about Sarabella. Some real bad dirt. Secrets he was keeping to himself."

"What were they?"

"Don said Cal wouldn't tell him, that he would have to find out for himself. He didn't want to get involved."

"So then why would he tell me anything now?"

"He liked Don, and now that he's dead, he might open up a little. It's a long shot, I know. I can't guarantee he'll tell you anything, but what the hell? You have nowhere else to go. Worth a try."

"I suppose."

"Do it. I have his address. I'll call him and set up a meeting."

I thought for a minute or so. Why not? Definitely a long shot.

Susan said, "I'll call him tomorrow."

After a long silence, I said, "But if he's got bad news for the Norbeck family, why are you so anxious for it to get out?"

"I hate her."

"Aw, come on. Knock it off."

"She calls me a slut."

"I don't believe that. Your mother loves you. She said so the other day. Said she adores you—wants only the best for both you guys."

"Coming from her, that's pure bullshit. She calls me a slut and worse. One time she called me a whore. I know damn well she's looking for the first excuse she can find to take me out of her will. Well, let's find out who's the real slut in this family."

Neither of us said anything for minutes. The loving was over.

Then an entirely naked Susan Norbeck got up out of bed without saying another word and walked to her room and slammed the door. I wondered why I was only now finding out just how fucked up the Norbeck family really was.

CHAPTER 25

COMPUTER SHOCK

When I walked into the dining room the next morning, Bertie, as had become ritual, was busy at the buffet, scrupulously preparing Sarabella's breakfast.

Susan was sitting at the table, starting on an English muffin. She said, as promised, that she had called Cal Bridges and set up my meeting with him. "He said he'd be happy to see you. After lunch." She then turned to the subject of Anne Reardon's computer phobia. "Bertie, you knew Anne Reardon hated the computer."

Bertie said without turning around, "I may have heard. I don't really remember."

"Sure you do. Remember how she always said she wouldn't go near one, afraid if she touched one, she'd wreck it?"

"If you say so, it must be true."

Susan issued an exasperated sigh. "Well, it is, and it means that Anne didn't kill him. Some professional did them both, and Paul is staying on to check it out."

Without so much as turning his head, Bertie pushed her hot button. "Maybe Legro had it done."

It worked. "That's a ridiculous stretch."

"No, it's not." Bertie turned to face her. "There was bad blood there. I heard Don and Ellie visited the Sin Club one time, and Legro put a move on Ellie, and Don pushed him. He made Legro look like an ass in his own club, so Legro had him killed."

"I was *at* that party," Susan yelled, "and it didn't happen that way.

Charles wouldn't do such a thing. He's a gentleman. Don was drunk. They were just talking."

"Yeah, but what were they talking about?"

"Nothing. You know Don was always jealous of guys coming on to her."

"I heard he pushed Legro so hard he fell over a couch and landed in someone's lap. He was pissed, and you know how vindictive Legro can be. Legro wasn't going to let that go away."

"He is *not* vindictive. He's a fine man. Don apologized, and Charles accepted it and forgot all about it."

"I don't believe Charles Legro would ever forget about it. I've seen how he operates. He always gets even, just not right away. He never forgets. He lets it simmer, but he never forgets. He's perfectly capable of killing Don."

Susan shook her finger at Bertie. "Charles Legro is a fine gentleman. Don apologized, and Charles forgot about it a long time ago."

Bertie said nothing—just rolled his eyes and turned back to the buffet. He folded a napkin, placed it on Sarabella's breakfast tray, and carried it out of the room.

Susan turned to me. "Bertie doesn't know what he's talking about. Charles is a gentleman."

"I heard you the first time."

"He would have accepted Don's apology like gentlemen do."

"Of course, dear." I wanted the discussion over. I had business with Ellie Norbeck.

An hour later, Ellie was sitting next to me at Don's computer screen when I reentered the revised password I'd discovered the day before. Don Norbeck's computer came to life again and asked me what I would like to see. I asked to see its list of documents, and a long list of files appeared on the screen. Most had working titles that made little sense to me. I skimmed down the list. The first title that did make sense was *The Sam Norbeck Story*. I gave it a click.

It didn't take long to realize that this file was what we were looking for: a manuscript in very rough draft form with all the misspellings and bad punctuation and grammar you would expect in a rough draft. A number of sentences, even paragraphs, were out of place. It would need a lot of editing to put it into publishable form. But it was readable. It told a lot about Sam Norbeck. I would come back to it when I had perused the remainder of the documents.

There were many files of research notes. One file contained reprints of newspaper articles detailing the police investigation into Sam's killing. Known gangsters in Detroit were quoted, as one would expect, flatly denying the killing. The articles said these were gangsters who would've bragged about knowing who killed him if they'd known who did it. Other files contained stories told by Sam Norbeck's friends he socialized with at Moorey's Grove. They were quoted as saying what a great guy Sam Norbeck was and how they couldn't believe someone would do this.

Another file had information that must have come from confidential police sources, telling how the crime had been investigated and why the police were so sure the job had been done by professionals, hired by a person or persons with deep pockets. There was general agreement that a lot of money changed hands when people were found who could pull off such a perfectly planned killing.

Other sources claimed to know how the assassination went down. Two men had to have arrived late at night by small boat, probably a small canoe or rowboat. Something quiet. The killer disembarked. The boat departed and returned the next day to retrieve him after the killing.

The assassin crept to the house, climbed the ivy on the east wall, entered a third-floor window, and hid himself until the next day. Apparently, a lot of research had gone into finding out that Sam would be home that afternoon. When Sam arrived home, the killer snuck up behind him, put a knife in his back, then ran to the boathouse, dove into the river, and allowed the strong current to carry him downstream to a waiting boat.

"It was only a guess," I said, "but Don could very well have gotten this information in confidence from our good friend Sergeant Chuck LaGrange."

Ellie nodded.

"Let's keep looking. So far, I don't see why Legro is so determined to get this computer, or even why Sarabella is so curious about what's in it."

"Let's try this file," Ellie said, pointing to one farther down the list. It was titled *Sin Club Fun*.

It turned out to be the mother lode. It contained pornographic videos produced at Club Sin. This had to be a Bertie Norbeck file—lots of detail how it was done, lots of video he had chosen not to show me. No way could Don have dug all this up.

We were less than a minute into a graphic porn video when Ellie shouted, "Close it, Paul. It's revolting. Turn it off." She looked away. There were tears in her eyes.

But I kept looking. Who knows, maybe I'm sicker than I realize. The file described in detail how Legro converted Sam's safe room into a studio to produce porn videos to an audience of very special club members. It showed Gitano and other club employees having their way with children. The porn was of the sickest kind—eight-year-olds who didn't know what was about to happen until it happened—even infants. A select audience from around the world, faces hidden, would watch and applaud.

"It's monstrous," Ellie said. "Who'd want to look at it?"

I didn't answer. I moved on and kept searching files. One file explained how the audience was carefully selected from a long list of "Executive" Sin Club members that indicated their addresses and countries of origin.

"I'm as amazed as you are," I said. "Look at this."

Ellie looked back at the screen.

"This file's got names of megamillionaires, bored inherited wealth, second-rate and has-been movie stars, dirty politicians, businessmen on expenses from China, Japan, Europe, Canada—from around the world. They all come here for high-stakes gambling and organized debauchery. This club is making huge profits for its parent company in Monaco."

Another file described how in addition to these disgusting entertainments, Mr. Charles Legro's Sin Club was a major entry point for humans, jewels, and drugs coming into and out of the United States. The Sin Club's limos and high-powered yachts cruised as far away as Toledo and Cleveland and parts of Canada. Their jet at the Grosse Ile Airport ranged even farther.

Then we came to Bertie. It was a file documenting how Bertie spied on Charles Legro's Sin Club. According to the file, Bertie had implanted miniature sensors in the building and hacked their computerized security video system. The file didn't go into much detail as to how he did it, but it sure as hell was information Legro didn't need to see.

Ellie said, "Do you suppose Bertie knows Don found out how he was spying on Legro?"

"I can't believe it. I think you have it backward. Don couldn't do it without his knowledge. He wasn't a computer geek. And I'm sure he would have mentioned it to him if he was. Bertie would have gone ballistic. It's more likely Bertie knows these files are on Don's computer. I think he gave Don these files as backup to hold in case anything happened to him. In which case, Bertie will do anything necessary to keep this computer safe. And I mean *anything*."

"Exactly what do you mean by *anything*, Mr. Steiger?"

"I mean, Bertie knows that public release of these files is his death warrant. I'm sure Legro's people have painful ways to make people disappear. Bertie will do whatever it takes to keep this file secure."

"You mean kill Don?"

"If he was worried Don might release it, why not?"

"So you're saying Bertie could have killed Don?"

"Doubtful. He had no reason to believe Don would release the file to anyone. If he did, he wouldn't have given him the file in the first place. Besides, he would never take the risk of killing him without securing the computer. So, for now at least, I have to doubt Bertie killed him. But he has to be very worried about what's going to happen to the computer."

"So what do we do now?" Ellie said. "These files are our death warrants too if Legro finds out we've seen them."

"If *anyone* finds out we've seen them, you can be sure it will get back to Legro."

"We tell no one, and then what?"

"Ellie, my dear friend and confidante, I suggest we download all these files to an empty thumb drive and stash it where it can be found only if we disappear. Then we delete all these toxic files from your computer, except maybe Don's manuscript, which has nothing of importance in it. When Legro returns, you reluctantly give it to him. Make him think you're scared he'll kill you. Let it slip out you seem to remember Don stashing a copy somewhere that may come to light. You don't know where it could possibly be. No need to give him the correct password. Let that be his problem. You don't want him to think you've gotten into the computer."

Ellie thought for a long moment. "You know what's odd about this whole thing is that Sarabella wants this computer as much as Legro does. What has her so uptight?"

"Well, I know one thing," I said. "Susan has been stirring her up about the book Don was writing, making her think it has depraved stories about the Norbeck family history. Hell, the title alone is enough to scare her if she's got something to hide."

"I can't imagine what that could be," Ellie said. "This town thinks the world of her."

"Yeah, I know."

Neither of us said anything for a minute, so I shut down the computer, stood up, and we headed back to her living room.

We were almost there when I abruptly stopped and turned to her. "Oh shit."

"What?"

"We're screwed."

"Why's that?"

"All that information we're going to delete from the computer—"

Ellie's sparkling blue eyes were wide open. "Yeah?"

"It's still on the backup drive you gave Gitano. They could crack the password accidentally just by misspelling my name. If they do, Bertie's fucked."

CHAPTER 26

CAL BRIDGES

After lunch, I headed toward Grosse Ile's *other* bridge, as they call it—the toll bridge at the north end of the island. I slowed to a stop to pay the toll, and soon I was in the town of Wyandotte, Michigan, on Biddle Avenue and looking for Columbine.

Other than at the funeral, I hadn't seen Cal Bridges in years. I remembered him well but had never known what he did for a living. He would occasionally show up at Moorey's and sit down with us guys for a beer. By now, he was into his late sixties, having been born a year after Sarabella. I liked Cal, and I know he liked Don. He was a low-key, pleasant guy, with three kids who had long ago left home and gone out into the world. Cal was retired now, and according to Susan, he and Kelli were enjoying their empty nest.

When I got to Columbine Avenue, my GPS indicated a left turn, and I continued west all through town to the western outskirts, where a fashionable real estate development of expensive homes had been constructed a few years back. The guard at the community gate let me pass, and I continued to Cal's home, a large single-story with attached two-car garage. It was off-white stucco over cinder block with a tile roof and had my kind of front yard—small, easy to cut, with few bushes to trim.

"Come on in, Paul," he said as he opened the front door. "Good to see you. The wife is away, so we can talk." Cal showed me to his study, returned from the kitchen with cold beers for both of us, and we settled into two comfortable chairs. He said he couldn't believe what had happened. Don was a great guy. He couldn't believe he would do such a thing.

"He didn't," I said. "I've been checking around, and it's looking more and more like murder. The cops are saying Dickie Reardon did it."

"Reardon?"

"Yeah. It was on TV last night."

He hadn't watched the news or seen this morning's paper, so I filled him in on why the police thought Dickie did it. "But they're wrong," I said. "There're some facts they don't have yet that prove someone else did it."

"Really. Wow." Cal paused to absorb it all. "So what can I do for you?"

"What I need from you is whether you can tell me anything that might help us find the real killer."

"Like what?"

"Like maybe a motive for killing Don. Why would anyone want to kill him?"

Cal sat back in his chair and looked away for a long moment. Then he looked back at me. "I can give you some family background that might be helpful, but you probably know a lot of that already. I doubt it will help much."

"Anything will help," I said. "Maybe ancient family background that isn't talked about today. Anything. For example, what were Sam and Marion really like?"

"They were wonderful people—had good values." Cal thought for a minute, then continued. "Sam was the grandfather I never had. He had a huge library in his home and kept after me to read the books in it every chance I could. I was thirteen when Sam died. I loved the man."

"Anything you can say about Don?"

Cal looked away. "Don came to me about six months ago for family background. He said he wanted to write a book about the Norbeck family, and I told him a little—mostly stories people already knew. I also told him there were stories I'd never tell anyone."

"Would Mattie know those stories?"

"She knows, but you'll never get her to tell you."

"Mattie told me she knew something. She called them black secrets. She got pretty shook up when she mentioned it."

"She'll never tell you anything. She has more respect for that Norbeck family than I do. Now that Don is dead, I can tell you a little more than I would've told him. But only a little."

"Anything you tell me will help."

"There are stories about the Norbeck family that I thought Don should never hear," Cal said. "Not only because he was writing a book and might repeat them but also because if he heard them, he'd probably never respect his mother and father again."

"That bad, eh?"

"Yup. If I tell you, you'll have to be very careful how you use it. If you repeat any of it, I'll of course deny it. Nothing in the story I'm going to tell you can be proved, and Sarabella will sue your ass off if you say anything. I'm only going to tell you if you promise to use it discreetly—only for background. Okay?"

Of course I agreed, and Cal proceeded to spellbind me. "During Prohibition, more booze came into the United States over the Detroit River than from any other source. Canada had Prohibition laws back then like the US, but their laws didn't prohibit exporting booze to the United States or anywhere else. By the early 1920s, huge amounts of illegal liquor were coming into the country over the river at night, much of it to Grosse Ile and over the bridges to Detroit. By then, Detroit's Purple Gang, an offshoot of the Mafia, had pretty much assumed control over the traffic."

I wondered where he was going with this.

"When he was a young guy, my dad worked for those guys."

"Doing what?"

"Driving boats full of booze over the river to Grosse Ile at night. He made a lot of money doing it."

I let him continue. His story didn't seem to be going anywhere, but I loved hearing old stories about my hometown.

"In winter, when the river froze over, he drove cars from Canada to Grosse Ile over the ice. Some years back then, the river would freeze over solid. If you knew where and when to look, you could see the headlights coming across the river. It was dangerous work. Sometimes cars fell through the ice."

"It's a great story, but I'm not sure this helps me."

"Wait," he said. "Let me continue."

I shut up.

"The guys Dad worked for were a brutal bunch and had thugs who ruthlessly enforced their rules. One in particular was Kiefer Ilyich."

"I may have heard that name somewhere."

"Kiefer married Molly Bunch. Molly was a colorful Detroit character."

"What do you mean by that exactly ... by *colorful*?"

"According to Dad, she was one of the better-known whores in Detroit in the twenties. When she quit the business, she ran a pawnshop next to the old Empress Theater on Woodward Avenue. Everyone in Detroit knew her. Died in 1950, some say of syphilis." He paused to take a swallow of beer, then added, "Kiefer was a very bad guy."

"How bad are you talking?"

"Let me put it this way: a couple of his victims died because they made fun of Molly. Kiefer's dead bodies generally ended up in the Detroit River and didn't resurface until the river current carried them out to Lake Erie. By then, the police'd lost interest."

"Some guy."

"I guess so. That's why Sam and Marion were so vehemently opposed to their son, Irwin, running around with Sarabella."

"Why's that?"

"Kiefer Ilyich was her father."

Cal let that settle for a moment while we both had some more beer.

"And ..." I prodded.

"Molly Bunch was her mother."

"Her mother?"

"So long as Sam drew a breath of air, Kiefer Ilyich and Molly Bunch were never going to be his in-laws."

I leaned forward, drained my beer bottle, then leaned back and waited for more.

"After Prohibition, Dad had trouble finding honest work. The Depression was big-time, and honest employers didn't want to screw with guys who couldn't account for their time during Prohibition."

"I can understand that."

"Then he got lucky. He met Sam Norbeck at Moorey's Grove one night. Sam was known to sample a few brews from time to time at Moorey's, and eventually he got to know my dad. They struck up a friendship, and when he heard Dad was out of work, he hired him as a bodyguard and chauffeur. Dad drove him everywhere. Put him to bed when he was drunk."

I nodded. "They got to be friends."

129

"Sam considered Dad a close friend, trusted him, and included him in his will. It was a very unusual will with a very important catch. Upon Sam's death, Dad would inherit a million dollars. But if Sam died violently, he would only get a hundred thousand. The reason, of course, was simple. It gave Dad every reason to keep him alive. And it's the very reason the police did not suspect him of Sam's murder."

"Must have been a shock to your dad when he found Sam dead."

"My father was profoundly shocked. He went to his grave believing professionals did it. He often said those killers came ashore from a small boat at night, got over the wall, then climbed the rose arbor on the east side of the house, grabbed on to those heavy cast-iron gutters, and swung in through a third-floor window. Sam usually kept several open in the summer to allow hot air to escape. There was no air-conditioning back then, as you know. Police noted signs of wear and stress on the ivy leaves and the gutters at the time, not realizing we kids caused it."

"I climbed that ivy more than once when I was a kid," I said. "So did Don."

"Dad said it was a dangerous time in Detroit in those days. Walter Reuther, shot in the arm with a shotgun in 1948. His brother, Victor, assaulted in 1949. Jimmy Hoffa disappeared in 1975. Dad used to say, 'Back then, you cross the line in Detroit, you die.' He said it many times." Cal let that sink in. "Now, I have one more story. One Dad never knew. Better open another cool one before I continue."

"Sure. I got all day."

Cal retrieved two more cold Budweisers from the kitchen, twisted the caps off, and handed one to me. He poured his beer and let the foam settle before continuing.

"Mattie doesn't know this one," he said. "Back then, she was working for Sam and Marion in the big house. On her days off, when Sam was in Detroit working and Marion was at her charity meetings and country club activities, I was thirteen at the time and would often be alone in the house afternoons, reading Sam's books in his library. Sometimes, Irwin would sneak Sarabella into the house, and they'd carry on upstairs like animals. At least they sounded like animals. I let 'em be. They never knew I was there."

I sat up in my chair. I wondered if it was the beer that had loosened Cal's tongue.

"Irwin was seventeen and Sarabella fourteen, and they hid their sex from Dad because they knew he'd tell Sam. My father was always in the guardhouse, so Irwin would bring Sarabella into the house through Sam's secret tunnel. He had the keys. You probably remember the tunnel's entrance was out in the west pasture where Dad couldn't see it from the guardhouse. It was disguised as a small horse barn."

"I remember hearing about it."

Cal Bridges continued with his version of Sam Norbeck's murder. It was different from what everyone else believed and really far out, and it didn't advance my investigation of Don's death. So I didn't listen closely. Anyway, it was getting late, and I had to get back to the Norbecks. Besides, I couldn't tell these stories to anyone. Cal would deny them. I'd wasted a full day.

I thanked Cal Bridges and returned to the Norbeck home disappointed.

Then I began to wonder if maybe there was a way to use Cal's stories after all.

Discreetly, of course.

CHAPTER 27

AUTOPSY

Back in my room, I got to work on a huge tuna fish sandwich and glass of milk Mattie had fixed for me. I was trying to think of a way to get that lethal backup drive away from Legro when the phone rang.

It was Sergeant LaGrange. "I'm calling from home and probably shouldn't be telling you this, but it's information I thought you should have. No need to spread it around until it's announced in the papers."

I gave him my word.

"There was an autopsy on Don Norbeck. We were keeping it quiet."

"Really. Why?"

"We were waiting for people to sound off. Maybe incriminate themselves."

"So why announce it now?"

"All the noise Sarabella's making. You know. The chief thought it would cool her down."

"And the results are carbon monoxide. Big surprise."

"That's right. As expected, carbon monoxide was found in Don's blood."

"So what's the big deal?"

Dead air for a few seconds. "There was something else."

"Yeah?"

"They found traces of cyanide."

"Oh my God."

"Someone poisoned him. Carbon monoxide gave Don the reddish tinge to the skin we saw in that photo. Turns out cyanide does that too."

I had to think about that for a few seconds. "What about the blow to the head? Could that have killed him?"

"The autopsy concludes the carbon monoxide killed him. If the blow to the head or the cyanide did it, you would expect to see little if any carbon monoxide in his blood because he wouldn't have been breathing it in."

"Makes sense."

"The blow on his head probably only stunned him. We saw little damage to the skull."

I had to stop and think. If the blow on the head had stunned Don, it was the cyanide in his blood that stunned me. I thought about the pictures of the crime scene Chuck had shown me. How in hell could cyanide have gotten into Don?

"Paul ... you still there?"

"Yeah, still here. Thinking. You remember that can of Coke on the bench? Could the cyanide have been put in the Coke?"

"There was some in it."

"And there was broken glass on the floor," I said. "Are you going to examine the glass for cyanide?"

"We did."

"And?"

"There were traces of cyanide on the glass."

I said nothing.

"Either Don was trying to make sure he would die, or else someone else was trying to make *damn* sure."

"So, was it murder or suicide?"

"Oh, it was murder, all right. Like we've been saying, his business partner did it. Reardon. It was a business fight. A squabble over money or some such. Happens all the time."

"Case closed?"

"Soon."

I looked away and smiled. It was a long moment before I came back at him. "You guys are dead wrong. Anne Reardon's confession on the computer is a phony, and you know it. She didn't even know how to turn one on, and you know that too."

"She'd figured out a way."

"I have good information that says she was scared of computers," I said. "She'd have handwritten the note if she wrote it."

"At a time like that, no one is thinking clearly. She went to the first thing she saw. She was probably in a hurry to kill herself. She wanted it over."

It was the usual cover-your-ass-with-both-hands theory that police departments came up with whenever they were out of answers and wanted to close a case. I couldn't believe my friend would stoop that low.

"Chuck, there're too many other possibilities. You got to look into them before closing the case."

"Sure, I'm going to go up to the chief and tell him he's full of shit. Keep the case open. And you know what he'll say."

"Go ahead and tell me."

"Chuck, clear out your desk and get the fuck out of here. Oh, and by the way, forget your pension." It was the first logical thing I'd heard him say.

"Reason with him."

"Ha … yeah, right. Paul, for Christ's sake, he doesn't want reason. He wants closed cases, and he's going to get one. Open cases cost money."

"He's going to be very embarrassed if he closes this one. I promise you that."

"I believe you've been told to lay off this case. More than once. You do not have the authority to investigate this murder. I suggest you get into your little red wagon and go back to Akron before your ass gets burned. You're sticking it out a country mile when you stick your nose into this shit."

"Aren't you interested in finding out who put cyanide in his drink?"

"Why would we care? It didn't kill him. Maybe Reardon put it in his Coke, hoping it would kill him. When it didn't, he popped him over the head and closed the garage door with the engine running. He knew that would kill him. Case closed."

"Sorry, Chuck. Case open, or else it should be. Take my word. There's more to this story than you know. Lots more. And it's going to come out. If I told you what I know right now, there would be more bodies for you to autopsy. Trust me when I say that. End of discussion. Goodbye."

He hung up before I finished talking, and I was glad. I didn't want him bringing me down to the station to get me to explain what I meant by "more bodies." If I told him, it would get to Legro. Bertie and I would disappear. Ellie, too, probably. Best case: I would be buried here in my hometown with all my arms and legs still attached.

CHAPTER 28

CYANIDE MEETING

The introduction of cyanide into the equation called for an emergency meeting of my kitchen cabinet that evening. But not at Moorey's. I wanted to run the confidential-for-now cyanide complication past them without Eric Gitano or anyone else jumping into the conversation at the wrong time. And particularly without mentioning anything about having opened Don's computer. That was going to have to remain a secret if Bertie, Ellie, and I were to stay alive.

Tom McGraw gladly volunteered his condo for the meeting. It was one of about two dozen single units on Grosse Ile that were to have been a gated community until funds for a fence around it and a guard station with uniformed guards at the entrance never materialized. The condominiums were well designed and very comfortable. Tom would never part with his two thousand square feet under air and attached two-car garage, in which he stored his one car beside an accumulation of valuable junk. It was all he needed to lead the life he wanted.

His condo came with two bedrooms connected to baths, a small office, and generous cabinet space in the kitchen devoted to a set of dishes and a wide range of beer, wine, and liquor for his guests, but mostly for him. One cabinet was devoted exclusively to his collection of Moorey's Grove inscribed glasses that were still half-full each time Jake Kubiak ordered him to leave at closing time. Several paintings on his walls appeared to have been salvaged from a motel scheduled for demolition. Opposite the liquor bar against the far wall was a fifty-five-inch flat-screen TV he seldom used except for football games and a dinner table perfect for conducting our business.

Joan arrived looking real good in a tight-fitting blouse and slacks. Her single strand of pearls and earrings added the perfect touch. Keeping my mind on business was going to be a problem.

When at last everyone was seated, I said to Bill and Joan, "Thanks for coming. I thought it might be better to have our meeting here rather than at Moorey's. We found out last Friday we can be overheard, and what I have to say is very private."

"What might that be?" Bill asked as we seated ourselves around the table.

I told them Ellie's story about Gitano threatening her and getting Don's external backup drive from her. I didn't mention we'd cracked the computer password.

"That's a load," Joan said. "I wonder if it's true. Anything else?"

"Lots. A very surprising autopsy report is out and not yet released. It found cyanide in Don's blood."

Joan's eyes widened. "Holy shit!"

"Yeah, holy shit. Apparently, it was in the open can of Coke on his workbench and on the broken glass on the floor."

"So was the killer killing him two ways?" Joan asked. "With carbon monoxide *and* cyanide?"

"The report says the cyanide didn't kill him. There wasn't enough in his blood. The carbon monoxide did it."

"The hell you say?" Bill said. "There was cyanide in his blood, but they're still going with carbon monoxide killing him?"

"How can they ignore the cyanide?" Tom asked.

I gave them Chuck LaGrange's explanation. "There's still no proof anyone else was there in that garage."

No one said anything.

"That's it," I said finally. "Case closed. They just want the murder to go away."

"I have a way to explain the cyanide," Joan said.

"How?"

"Charles Legro ordered Don killed after Susan told him the title of

Don's book. The title, all by itself, spooked him. It lit up his imagination. It scared him shitless. He took twenty grand off Susan's bar bill."

"And had Gitano kill him," I filled in.

"Yeah. He orders Gitano to kill him. Gives him some cyanide. Tells him to poison him. Make it look like suicide."

Tom shook his head and sat back in his chair.

Joan glared at him. "Come on. It could work. Gitano goes to Don's house, finds him in his garage working on his car. Asks for the computer. Don refuses. Don turns his head for a minute, and Gitano slips cyanide into his Coke." Joan glanced around with a satisfied look on her face.

"Good theory," Bill said, "but there's no proof Gitano was there. Plus, you said yourself Gitano would have to have taken the computer itself if Legro had ordered it done. And somehow, I don't see Legro and cyanide in the same picture. Too girlie. I can't visualize a thug like Gitano casually dropping a pinch of cyanide in Don's drink, which by the way wasn't enough to kill him, and then continuing on with a conversation until Don sips his Coke and keels over."

"It's not impossible," Joan said.

"Legro uses poison *and* carbon monoxide to dispose of people?" I said. "Sorry. I say Legro's enemies just disappear."

We were silent for several minutes as we thought about how cyanide could be explained at the scene of a death by carbon monoxide.

Then Joan sat up in her chair. "Reardon didn't do it. Reardon isn't a cyanide kind of guy. Anne Reardon made up the story in her note to justify killing a husband she hated. Gitano didn't do it, because we agree he would've taken the computer, not only the drive. The cyanide says it was a premeditated hit. So that says it has to be one of Sarabella's kids that did it. Maybe both of them."

"How do you figure?" I asked.

"It's not about the book—or the computer. It's about money."

"Okay," I said. "Go on."

"We know her kids don't get along. And we know Sarabella's threatened to dispossess their lazy asses for years using Don with his power of attorney. They suspect Don is colluding with Sarabella to inherit all her money when she's gone. We've heard that often enough. Bertie and Susan had finally had enough, got together that day, and went over to confront Don about their inheritances with a supply of cyanide probably already loaded into a can of Coke."

"Where would they get the cyanide?" Tom asked.

"Who knows? They found it somewhere. So they go over to his home. That day, they were in luck. He was alone in his garage working on his car with the engine running. Ellie was away somewhere. It was a perfect setup."

"Okay so far," Bill said. "What happens next?"

Joan continued. "At first, they're all buddy-buddy. They chitchat and admire the car. Don's halfway through checking his transmission oil level and about to add a little more when they offer him the Coke. He thanks them, says it's welcome on such a hot day, takes a swig, and doubles over in pain. He falls to the floor and hits his head. Or maybe they tap him when he goes down. Either way, he's out cold on the floor."

"So what do they do then?" Tom said.

"The car engine is still running. They just back away and walk over to the door closer and push the button. They exit the garage through the house and out the front door. Don's computer is not an issue for them, so it stays put."

Bill nodded. "That could work."

Tom looked at Bill. "They were taking a hell of a chance that no one saw them there."

"I agree," Bill said, "but they would've checked to make sure no one was around."

"Turns out the Reardons were home," Tom said.

"Yeah, but they couldn't have seen them from any of the windows in their house," Bill said. "Their windows don't give a view into the garage."

Joan added, "Bertie's smart enough to know it's not unusual for sons to commit suicide in the same manner as their fathers. That's been reported from time to time. It's fairly common knowledge now. So he reasons that the authorities will call it a suicide."

"Which is what they did," Tom said.

"What do you think, Paul?" Bill asked.

"How does Bertie account for his time?" I said. "He and Susan have to have an alibi."

Joan smiled. "Bertie has that computer room of his. He's a computer wizard. He could easily produce fake proof of where he and Susan were that afternoon. Hell, he could probably fake evidence that Gitano was over there and killed him. I'll bet he could place fake evidence of a cyanide purchase by the Sin Club somewhere in their files to divert attention from him. They would never suspect him or Susan."

We sat in silence for many minutes, trying to add to or subtract from our theories, but couldn't.

Finally, Bill reached for his drink and drained it. "I got work tomorrow. How about you guys?" He stood up to leave.

I wasn't comfortable ending the meeting just yet and motioned for him to sit back down, which he did, slowly. Something about the theories we'd thrown out on the table so far bugged me. Something was missing. Why, if Bertie was guilty of this, had he been so helpful and open to me? And why didn't he take the computer? They didn't know it, but for him, it was an extremely important issue. He had a life to lose if it was opened.

Then I thought of someone we'd overlooked.

CHAPTER 29

SARABELLA

"I think we have one more suspect to consider."

"Who?" they all asked in unison.

"Sarabella."

There was silence in the room for a few seconds while they looked around at each other.

Joan shook her head. "She wouldn't kill her own son."

"Why not?" I said. "Cyanide is more of a woman's way of killing. Men are more hands-on—guns, knives, garrotes, you know, that sort of thing."

Tom looked at the others. "Yeah, but the cyanide didn't kill him."

"I know she was there that afternoon."

"How can you know that?" Bill asked.

"She said so at her dinner party. She said Reardon was home that day cutting his lawn. I doubt she could have known that unless she was there. I'd ruled Sarabella out as a suspect because she's too fragile to have brought Don down with a blow to the head. But she's not too fragile to hit a man prostrate on the ground from cyanide." I waited a few seconds to let that sink in and looked around at them. "And let's face it. It would have been easy for Sarabella to kill Don."

"How?" asked Tom.

"Like this," I said. "Sarabella goes to visit Don and finds him in his garage. She has a cyanide pill in her purse and a can of Coke in a small handheld cooler. The garage door is open, and he's working on his car. He's hot and sweaty. She offers him a cold Coke. He accepts. They get into an argument over the book. Don again refuses to stop the book—and

140

again tries to explain to his mother she will love the book. But Susan has poisoned her mind. Sarabella has secrets she cannot allow out in public under any circumstances. Finally, she gives up and, in a fit of utter desperation, puts the cyanide in Don's Coke. He sips the Coke. He doubles up in pain, slips on the oil on the floor, and falls. He is stunned when he hits his head. She thinks he's dead."

"She walks out of the garage and closes the garage door," Tom said.

For a minute, no one said anything.

I broke the silence. "But there's a catch."

"The catch being?"

"Maybe she closes the door, maybe she doesn't." I paused to let that sink in.

They just looked at me, so I continued.

"If she didn't close the door, she didn't kill Don. It's only attempted murder. If you talk with her about it, you can be sure she will deny closing the garage door. She'll deny even being there, and how the hell would you prove she was there unless a witness turns up some day? She'll say she heard Reardon tell her he cut his lawn that day. The Reardons are dead, so they can't deny it."

There was another long silence.

"Why Sarabella?" Bill asked. "Why not Susan?"

"Why not Anne Reardon?" Tom said.

"Because Sarabella was there at the garage that afternoon, and she has a big motive. We have no evidence that Susan, Bertie, or Reardon were there."

"What big motive?" Joan asked. "How could she have had a strong enough reason to kill her own son? I just can't believe that's possible."

I nodded. "Trust me. She's got one. A big one. Remember, Susan had told her Don was writing a book about the Norbecks and that she wouldn't like what he was putting in it. It was only a lie to upset her mother, of course, with Susan little realizing how *much* it upset her. Do any of you know anything about Sarabella's background?"

"No," Bill said. "She never mentions it."

"Suppose she never mentions it for a very good reason—a very, *very* good reason. Suppose it's some terrible secret of hers that she can't under any circumstance allow to be revealed."

Joan sat back in her chair, folded her arms, and looked down. "I can't believe a mother would kill her own son. No way."

I looked at Joan. "Think about the title of Don's book. With a title like that, the reader expects it's about something bad. Very bad. If she's got secrets that must not under any circumstance be revealed, think what her imagination may have spawned. Sarabella's imagination could have gone every bit as wild as Legro's did."

Joan, still looking down, shook her head. "Sure, but to kill her own son?"

"The cyanide was a last resort," I said. "Only if she couldn't talk Don out of writing his book."

"So," Bill said, "you think Susan had conned her mother into believing Don was going to destroy her family?"

"I surely wouldn't put it past Susan. She's already conned Legro out of twenty thousand dollars."

"I'm still not ready to believe this about Sarabella," Joan said.

"Why not Dickie Reardon?" Tom said. "The police think he did it. Anne killed him because he killed Don. The cops are closing the case."

"Maybe he did do it," I said. "But he doesn't have much of a motive to commit *murder*. Why would he *kill* Don?"

Joan waved a hand in the air and looked at me. "Hold on a minute, everybody. Big question. If Sarabella had killed him, why would she ask you to investigate? Why not let Don's death be a suicide?"

"I wondered when you guys would get around to that question. And it's a good one. Why would she pick me? Why not a professional?"

"Or no one?" Bill said.

"When she first called me, I begged her to find a private detective to look into Don's death. She refused. She wanted me. So the question nagged me, and I thought about it a lot. I finally came up with these reasons. It's a long answer, so bear with me. Reason one: Sarabella wanted people to know she'd solicited me to find out who did it and therefore believe she could not have done it herself."

Joan raised her hand. "Why did she wait four days after Don's death to call you to tell you he was dead?"

"Why? Because it was only then she'd heard I was back from Europe. By then, she was worried. She couldn't be sure she hadn't been seen at

Don's garage that afternoon. Reardon could have seen her at the garage, and she knew he wouldn't keep his mouth shut if he had. The thought occurred to her that insisting I, an amateur investigator, investigate, and as such unlikely to find anything important, gives her the appearance of innocence. She could've thought that as Don's best friend and a veteran of Iraq, I could reason with Reardon—persuade him that saying anything about her would be unwise."

"Okay, so what else?" Joan asked.

"It was important that I attend her very special party with that unusual combination of guests after the funeral. She wanted me at the party to know whom I was to suspect, to hear her accuse everyone she knew who had opportunity and motive—*except* her and her kids—especially *not* her kids. I was there to hear her tell me one of the others at the party could have murdered Don."

"Why should she suspect Ellie?" Joan asked.

"Sarabella's recollection may have been that when she walked away from the garage, she'd left the garage door open and the car engine running. When she heard rumors of suicide by carbon monoxide, she realized she hadn't killed him and began to imagine Ellie had found Don unconscious, not dead, when she returned home, and had closed the garage door to kill him and make it look like suicide. Almost too easy. Ellie had two motives. They'd been fighting, and big-time money. Sarabella included Ellie on her dinner list of suspects so I would meet her. As Don's best friend, she believed I would be more likely to find evidence implicating Ellie than some outside private eye."

"So, is that it? That's why she wanted you here?" Tom said.

"No. There is another reason for me being here, maybe the most important reason. She wants me to get to Don's computer and delete its files. I'm the only one she could depend on to do it for her. Sarabella fears that if that computer gets into the wrong hands, it could be the basis of blackmail, costing her millions and ruining the family reputation."

There was a silence while they took it all in.

I broke the silence. "And, last of all, she believes, as a loyal family friend, I will delete any evidence harmful to her, Bertie, or Susan."

Joan leaned forward and looked at me. "Would you do that?"

"I don't know," I said. "I really don't know what I'd do if I found out someone in her family killed Don."

No one said anything.

Then I said something I'd been thinking about for some time. "Sarabella has threatened over the years to disinherit Bertie and Susan, hoping to stimulate in them a drive to succeed that just isn't there. Instead, she inspired the dread of facing life without family money. The Norbeck family is so dysfunctional that Bertie and Susan, born without a scintilla of inner drive to succeed, expecting family money to carry them through life, cannot imagine their mother could love and protect them. Either or both of them could have killed Don."

<hr />

I got back to the Norbeck home late and tired. Susan's door was wide open, the room empty. I didn't care, but I did wonder where she was. Turns out Susan was in my bed, stripped for action.

"Missed you last night," I said as I pulled off my clothes and headed to the bathroom.

"Paul, I think I've fallen for you again. Deeply. I needed time to think it over. I'm all mixed up. I hope you'll forgive me."

"Consider yourself forgiven," I said from the bathroom, rolling my eyes as I started to brush my teeth.

When I returned to the bedroom, she asked, "What did Cal tell you? Anything that will help?"

"Nothing you don't already know."

The look on her face told me she didn't believe me. But it didn't diminish the loving that followed.

CHAPTER 30

BERTIE

I arrived at the breakfast table the next morning shortly after nine, dragging my butt. It had been a heavy workout the night before, with little sleep. Susan had gone to her room in the early morning and hadn't reappeared.

Bertie was at his usual station at the buffet. His back was to me. Without looking, he said, "Good morning, Paul. Good sleep?" I knew he was smiling when he said it.

"Had trouble getting to sleep last night for some reason."

Then, out of pure curiosity, I walked over to the buffet to inspect his careful preparation of Sarabella's breakfast and pour myself a coffee from the pot he had just used for Sarabella's. I stared. He was carefully counting out individual silver-gray crystals from a small container and putting them one by one in her coffee.

"What's that?"

"Mother insists on a very special sweetener. Says it helps her digestion."

"What is it?"

"I'm not sure," he said.

I decided to try a pinch and reached over for some. "If it's good enough for her, it must be great."

"Get away from there. That's not for you." He pushed my arm away with some force before I could reach the sweetener.

Now I was curious. "Why so rude, Bertie? What the hell is that shit?"

He dropped another crystal into Sarabella's coffee cup. "None of your business. Go on back to the table. There's plenty of sugar over there."

"Tell me what that is."

"I don't have an exact name for it. It's just something Mother wants."

"Your mother know you're putting that shit in her coffee?"

"Go back to the table, Paul."

"You son of a bitch." I seized his arm, sending what was left of the grains in his hand across the top of the buffet. "That's cyanide, isn't it? You're putting cyanide in her coffee. You son of a bitch."

"It's not what you think." Bertie hurried to brush the spilled granules back into his hand.

"You're a goddamned animal."

"It won't kill her," he said, his voice on the rise. "I'm not trying to kill her."

My God, he didn't deny it. "If not kill, what the hell else? What is that shit?"

He put both hands up in front of him. "Calm down, calm down. I'm not going to tell you till you calm down."

I calmed down slowly and finally said, "Okay. I'm calm. Now tell me what this is all about."

"When Don died, Mother got hyper. She started acting crazy. She was shouting crazy things. Accusations. She was telling people I'd killed Don. She didn't know what she was saying, and saying it to anyone who would listen. I had to do something to cool her down. This was the first thing I could think of."

"But cyanide is a poison, for Christ's sake."

"Hey, I only put enough in to calm her down. I had a college professor once show me how to do it. The amount used has to be carefully measured. Too much and it will kill—like you say. But keep to a limited amount, and Mother calms down. It's called cyanide poisoning. No big deal. Workers around plastics, chem labs, landfill, and waste sites get it all the time. It's not uncommon. She gets a headache, feels nausea, and her balance is off a little. And she sleeps a lot. She's so fuzzy now no one listens to her ravings."

"Bertie, you're a fucking animal to do that to your mother. Knock it off."

"I'm telling you, it won't hurt her. And as soon as the police make a final determination of how Don died, I'll back off. I'll taper off slowly. She'll be fine."

"Bertie, you're stopping now. This is insanity. Either you back off or I'm telling her."

"Goddamn it. Keep out of this!" He paused to draw a calming breath. "Let me explain something. When Don died, Mother started spouting off about Don's computer and what she thought was in it. Susan has conned her into believing it had stories about her early life and that it had to be opened and the files erased. But for me, it's different. You remember what I told you about Legro's operation? A copy of my computer file describing it is on Don's computer."

"So?"

"If that computer is opened, I'm a dead man, and anybody who looks at it is dead."

I didn't like that answer at all. I didn't think he needed to know Ellie and I had seen it and that Legro had Don's backup drive.

He continued. "After Mother's party, I had to confuse her to the point no one would listen to her about opening Don's computer."

"How the hell did your file get onto Don's computer in the first place? Did you put it there?"

"Yeah, I put it there."

"Why, for God's sake?"

"I put it there so it would be preserved if anything happened to me or my computer. I was the one in danger—not Don."

"Why put it on *Don's* computer? Why not somewhere else?"

"He was the only one I knew I could trust. I never imagined anything would happen to *him*. He was living a perfectly normal life. No enemies. Good friends. I thought his computer was safe."

I started to add a little sugar to my coffee. Then I thought better of it, put the spoonful back in the sugar bowl, set the spoon down, carefully put the top back on the sugar bowl, and moved it aside. I looked back at Bertie. "Well, anyway, Bertie, stop or I'm telling her. There are other ways to protect what's on that computer. We can delete the files on the computer and store them somewhere else."

I could see he was pissed. He gave me a look that could kill, then dumped Sarabella's coffee and poured a new one. I watched him put real sugar in it. Then he picked up the tray, looked at me, and said, "Don't you even think about saying one goddamned word to anyone," before walking out of the room.

I returned to the dining table, poured myself a glass of orange juice, and sat down, stupefied. What in the world could he have been thinking?

Part of the story was coming together now. Over the years, there'd been time for Bertie to have stumbled across that old bottle of cyanide his father had used on himself. Maybe Sarabella had used some of it to hurry Marion along to her heavenly reunion with Sam. Who knows?

Now I saw a new Bertie—a Bertie who, if his mother didn't eventually back off her accusations or her threats to remove him from her will, could contemplate gradually increasing her cyanide dose, knowing the authorities would understand the passing of an elderly society matron, especially after the shock of losing a beloved son. He would get away with it. Poisoners often did. I sat there at the breakfast table slowly shaking my head. I had learned the Norbecks were a family of poisoners beginning with poison for Irwin's suicide, if it had been suicide.

I finished the orange juice and went back to the buffet to pour myself another cup of coffee. Black. No sugar.

Mercifully, Mattie came in from the kitchen right then. "Here're your eggs, Paul, scrambled, the way you like them. Call if you need anything."

"Thanks, Mattie," I said. "You're just in time. You've saved my life." I wondered again as she walked out if she'd heard any of the conversation between Bertie and me. I hoped not.

The room was quiet now, and I had time to think. I was nearly finished with breakfast and into my third cup of coffee when an idea occurred to me. How to get Sarabella to confess to killing her favorite son. Lie through my teeth.

It would have to be this afternoon, before this evening's dinner with Susan at the Sin Club.

CHAPTER 31

CONFESSION IS GOOD
FOR THE SOUL

"Sarabella, how're you feeling?" I asked as I knocked on her open bedroom door.

"Come in, Paul. I'm feeling much better, thanks. The headache's almost gone."

"I wanted to let you know I've made a little progress and thought maybe you'd want to be brought up to date."

"By all means. Come in. Sit down."

I entered, gently closed the door, and sat in the plush, overstuffed chair that faced her on her side of the bed. She was sitting back against several pillows that some nice person had plumped up behind her. There was color in her face now, and she held her head up without the support of an index finger against her temple. I knew why she was feeling better. If I'd told her, she'd have disinherited Bertie in a nanosecond.

"Can I get you anything before we begin?"

"Nothing, thanks. Let's get started."

"I don't think you know that an autopsy was performed on Don."

She leaned forward and stared at me. "No. I didn't. Why do it? The carbon monoxide killed him."

"True enough, Sarabella, but something was found in his body that leads me to add one more person to my list of suspects."

"What something?"

"Cyanide."

She leaned her head back on the pillow, looked at the ceiling, and thought about that for a long moment. "Whom do you suspect?"

I hesitated for a few seconds, wondering if this would work. It was the last bullet in my gun. Looking directly at her, I said, "You."

Her eyes darted to me for a second and away for longer before returning to me, and then away again. She fussed nervously with a wrinkle in her flowered nightgown and then smoothed it over with a quick motion.

I'd hit a nerve. I hated what I was doing to this fine lady, and now there was no turning back. "You could've killed him."

Finally, her lips formed a crooked smile, and without looking directly at me, she whispered, "You're not serious. You know I could never kill one of my children."

I was not smiling. "I find it almost impossible to believe, Sarabella, but I have to put you on my list."

"How could I do such a thing?"

"The how is easy. You were there at his garage that afternoon."

"How could you believe that?" She was sitting up now, and her replies came quickly. She had found a source of energy trapped animals find when faced with danger.

"You admitted as much when you said at your dinner party that Reardon was home that afternoon. I believe you said he was cutting his lawn. You had no way of knowing that unless you'd visited Don that afternoon."

Her eyes flared. "Of course I did. He told me at my party he was home cutting his lawn."

"Sorry, but no he didn't. The subject never came up that evening. Remember? I was there."

"Even if it didn't, your logic is preposterous. How could you go from me being there to me killing him?"

"Easy. The cyanide in Don's blood. You put it in his Coke. Then he doubled over in pain and slipped on the oily floor. Maybe he hit his head when he fell or maybe you hit him over the head with something. Doesn't matter. Then you walked out and closed the door."

Sarabella stifled a sob. "How could you think such a thing? I loved Don. I love my kids too much to do such a thing."

"Oh, you could do such a thing, all right. How do I know? I've opened Don's computer. I've seen what's in it."

"Like what?"

"There are some very wild and very true stories in it."

"I don't believe it."

"You killed him because he refused to destroy his book."

"No."

"You killed him to keep those stories in his book from becoming public."

"No."

"You killed him because you knew those stories about you and your mother and father were true."

"My mother and father?"

"Who your mother was and how she died."

"How she died?"

"Yes. Of syphilis."

"That's a lie."

"Your secrets are out now, Sarabella. There are no more secrets."

"I have no secrets!" she shouted. "I've never had secrets."

"About your mother and father?"

"No."

"About Irwin?"

"No."

"About Marian Norbeck?"

"No."

"About Sam Norbeck?"

"No!"

"I think you do."

"What the hell do my mother and father have to do with anything?"

"You believed Don was putting stories about them in his manuscript."

"No."

"Smiley Bridges knew your father, and you knew he didn't like him."

"My father?"

"Yes. Kiefer Ilyich."

"What about him?"

"You knew Smiley Bridges told Sam your father worked for the Purple Gang in Detroit during Prohibition."

"No."

"Said he was sly and dangerous."

"Not true."

"You know it's true."

"No."

"You know Smiley told Sam your father had murdered people. More than one. You know that's true too."

"No."

"You also know the story of a woman in Detroit who ran a pawnshop on Woodward Avenue next to the old Empress Theater. You'll do anything to hide that story."

"I know of no such woman."

"She was your mother. Molly Bunch. Smiley Bridges knew her too. Knew she was a hooker before she retired and ran the pawnshop. A famous hooker. She married Kiefer Ilyich, and they moved to Grosse Ile. Died young of syphilis. It's where you get your good looks."

"No."

"It's why Sam didn't want you to marry his only son."

Sarabella flinched. She sank back into her pillows, looked at the ceiling, and screamed, "I did not kill Don! I didn't. I had no reason to kill my son."

"Oh, you had reason, Sarabella, a very strong reason," I said, trying my best to remain calm. "I haven't gotten to the best part yet. Don's computer says you killed Sam Norbeck and tells exactly how you did it."

"No."

"With a letter opener in the middle of his back. Irwin was there when you did it."

Sarabella slowly shook her head, but her face said yes, that Cal's story was true. There was no longer any doubt in my mind now, and I continued with the story she'd convinced herself was in Don's book since she'd first learned the title. To her, the title of the book said it all. There was no other possibility. It was a story she had to kill for.

"There's more," I said.

Sarabella looked away.

"You realized Don had found out you killed Sam and was putting it in his book."

Her face was completely drained now. Other than a slight tremor in her fingers, she didn't move.

"Back in 1960, when you and Irwin were teenagers, you snuck past Smiley Bridges to get in the house and make out, as they used to say back then. This went on for over a year. Irwin had it down to a science. You entered the house through Sam's escape tunnel. Irwin had a key and knew Smiley couldn't see the entrance from where he sat in the security office at Sam's iron gate. Any afternoon Marion was away, you were free to spend in Irwin's bedroom on the second floor. It was a perfect setup."

Sarabella started to say something, but I motioned I wanted to continue.

"Let me explain how and why you killed Sam that afternoon."

"Go ahead." Sarabella was still looking away, hands beside her flat against the mattress.

"On the day of Sam's death, after sex with Irwin, you walked downstairs and were shocked to find that Sam Norbeck had unexpectedly come home. He was on the phone. His back was to you. He was hard of hearing, so he wouldn't have heard you. He was telling his lawyer to change his will so all his money would go to charity if Irwin, his only son, married you."

Sarabella didn't move. Just looked away.

"Infuriated and without thinking, you looked around, saw a letter opener, seized it, crept up behind Sam, and stuck it in his back just as he hung up the phone. Sam ran toward his safe room with the letter opener in his back and collapsed. It must have nicked an artery because there was a trail of blood. All that blood made it look like there'd been a struggle. You walked to the body, bent over, and wiped your fingerprints from the handle. Then you ran back upstairs, told Irwin what you'd done, and the two of you raced out of the house in panic through the tunnel. Irwin was now an accessory to the murder of his father and completely under your control. And you made sure he knew it."

Sarabella, still looking away, said nothing.

"Smiley Bridges found Sam's body hours later. He had records of Mattie, Sam, Marion, and Irwin leaving the house in the morning and no record of anyone other than Sam returning before he was killed. Smiley may have suspected you and Irwin were sneaking into the house behind his back, but he didn't mention this to the police because it was only a suspicion. There was no reason for him to believe you were in the house on that particular day."

Sarabella started to say something but then closed her mouth without speaking.

"Irwin was horrified at what had happened, and you threatened him with exposure, that you would say he did it if he didn't promise to marry you. Of course he married you. Irwin was now saddled with an unbearable burden, the reason for his later suicide."

Sarabella did not interrupt me.

"Irwin kept saying for years after Sam's death that he couldn't bear the guilt and wanted to confess. It wasn't long before you began to think it might be better for the family if Irwin died. He didn't have your inner strength, Sarabella. You could see he wasn't setting Sam's murder aside like you had. He was showing signs of depression. You were afraid he was giving in. I can imagine him telling you he couldn't sleep. He might've mentioned suicide to you."

"He did," she said quietly, still looking away. "Several times."

"So you obtained cyanide tablets and put them where Irwin could find them. Seeing them, he would begin to see a way out. Whether you convinced him to take the cyanide or whether you added cyanide to his coffee is a question I can't answer. Anyway, one way or another, Irwin finally ingested the cyanide. To the authorities, it was an obvious suicide."

Sarabella slowly shook her head.

"Sarabella, either you poisoned your husband or else gave him cyanide pills and encouraged him to take them. There is no question you encouraged him to relieve his burden."

She did not reply, so I kept on.

"Another question that bothers me is whether you used those same cyanide tablets on Marion after she moved into your home."

Sarabella again slowly shook her head, and her eyes moistened.

"It's a question that'll never be answered," I said. "But now that you were familiar with cyanide, it's easy to imagine you poisoned Marion to hasten your inheritance. You would have placed small amounts of cyanide in her coffee, gradually increasing the dose until Marion died what looked like a natural death. An expert recently showed me how."

That did it. She rolled over facedown on the bed and sobbed into her pillow. It was a long time before she rolled back, wiped her eyes, and faced me.

"After Prohibition ended, the gangs broke up," she said. "What was left of the gangs in Detroit didn't want my dad around, and he couldn't find honest work. He never recovered from the end of Prohibition. After Mother died, there was barely enough money to put food on the table." Sarabella wiped her eyes.

"Take your time."

"My father told me over and over again how supremely important it is to have money, to get money any way you can. I saw how my father struggled back then. Paul, we didn't even have a bathtub. I took baths standing bare-ass beside the kitchen sink until I was fifteen.

"By the time I was a teenager, I knew I was going to get out of poverty any way I could. I didn't care how. When Irwin showed interest in me, I determined I would marry him for the Norbeck money. It was my way out of my family filth. When I overheard Sam telling a lawyer to change his will, I blanked out. I acted without thinking." Her eyes finally met mine. "Paul, you have to believe me. I didn't understand what I'd done until Irwin dragged me out of the house through that tunnel. I've always thought Smiley Bridges suspected me, but he never gave me away. Probably because he didn't want to involve Irwin. So I made sure the Bridges family was well taken care of after Irwin died."

"Smiley never suspected the truth."

"I'm not sure," she said softly, now avoiding my eyes. "I think he might have. I always wondered if maybe his son, Cal, was in the library that day and saw what happened. Sometimes he went there to read. He'd have told his father."

"If Cal had seen you kill Sam, he would've been a fool to tell his father or anyone else, because if he admitted being there, police would have suspected him of the killing. Besides, if he'd told his father, Smiley wouldn't have believed it for a minute. He would've refused to believe it. He was convinced from his years in the Purple Gang during Prohibition that Sam's death was a professional kill, not something that could be done by some wild teenager. No way he'd have believed you did it."

Sarabella's eyes were still very moist. "Smiley never bothered to record Cal's comings and goings. He knew his son was a good boy. It wouldn't have occurred to him that Cal did it."

We sat there, neither of us saying anything or looking at the other for a long time.

Finally, Sarabella looked over to the window and said in almost a whisper, "Paul, you have to understand, I had to kill Don. I could never have allowed him to print that stuff about my family. I just couldn't. I wasn't thinking straight. And it was so easy. Just a small pill in Don's Coke. It was so easy … so quick. He took one sip, doubled up, slipped on the oil, and it was over. I just walked away."

We sat there some more, letting what she had said sink in. She dabbed at her eyes with her handkerchief.

"And closed the garage door," I said.

She thought for a few seconds, looked over to me, and said, "Hell no. Why would I? He was dead."

I thought about the door, and somehow I believed her. I think it was the way she said it. So matter-of-fact. Not appreciating the importance of it. That she believed she'd killed her son, but what she said meant she hadn't. I believed her. She hadn't killed Don.

Anyway, there would be no way in hell I or anyone could prove any of it. None of this was in Don's computer, of course. It was the shocking story Cal had revealed to me yesterday. Word of mouth. That's all it was. Cal had sworn me to secrecy, and of course Cal would vigorously deny any and all of it if I let it out.

This was Sarabella's private hell. That's all it was. A private hell she'd lived in all these years, day and night since Sam and Irwin had died, and would continue to live in until the day she died.

I slowly leaned back in my chair, looked at her, and waited.

Finally, she looked over to me and frowned. "What?" she yelled.

"Why so upset?"

"What the *hell* do you mean?" she growled, almost coming up out of her bed.

"I'm not going to say anything. I'm your friend. Besides, no one's going to see what's in Don's book. It reads like a ninety-nine-cent Kindle murder mystery. It reads like crap. Computers have a delete key for a reason."

Sarabella leaned back against her pillows. Unlike the Sarabella I'd known since I was four years old, she couldn't think of a thing to say.

Her eyes and mouth were still wide open when I got up out of my chair and left the room. She seemed to realize that the dreadful secrets buried in her soul for so many years would remain there. I walked down the hall to my room, wondering how long it would take Sarabella to get that shocked look off her face.

I stretched out on the bed to think. I wasn't going to solve Don's murder. Sarabella Norbeck didn't do it. Dick Reardon didn't do it. Legro and Gitano could have done it, but there wasn't any proof. The real killer, somewhere out there in the black space between theory and conjecture, was nothing more than a wild-ass guess.

I worried what would happen if Legro ever opened the portable hard drive Ellie had given him. But that would be Bertie's problem. Ellie would have to tell him sooner or later that she'd given it to him.

As for me, I'd struck out. All I'd done was piss people off and make things worse. The grotesque cancer on Grosse Ile's east shore three hundred yards north of Sarabella Norbeck's home would grow and metastasize. It would get ugly. I didn't want to be there when it popped.

CHAPTER 32

DINNER AT THE SIN CLUB

I had finished tying the one tie I'd brought with me when Susan stepped in the door.

"Let's go," she said.

"Let's go." The well-worn sports jacket I was going to wear was still on the back seat of my car where I'd thrown it after Sarabella's dinner party, and I knew that sometime during the evening, Susan was going to mention that it didn't match the tie or my trousers. We headed downstairs and out the door to my car for the short run to the Sin Club.

I put on my jacket and got in.

Susan said, with only the faintest of smiles, "When are you going to get a new one?"

"A new jacket?"

"No. A new car."

"When this one wears out," I said. "Thanks for the compliment." Not a good start to the evening.

"Just kidding," she said, but I didn't think she was.

It took only a couple of minutes to get over to the Sin Club from the Norbeck home, and when we got there and stopped in front of the huge wrought iron gate with its outrageous initials, it grudgingly opened. Susan said some kind of an automated security system opened it when we drove up.

I said, "No shit." Definitely a bad start to the evening.

Ignoring my comment, she said, "Park at the front door rather than that parking lot just beyond. No one will bother it there."

We passed through the gate. It closed behind us, and I parked where she said to park.

I had seen the estate after Sam's death on my several surreptitious visits with friends many years ago, and again the other morning from a distance through Bertie's telescope. But up close, it was always awesome. Sam Norbeck had ordered his architect to outdo the Grosse Ile mansions of other automotive high rollers. William Knudsen of General Motors, Ransom E. Olds, inventor of the Oldsmobile and Reo trucks, Ford's Harry Bennett, and other lesser-known automotive bigwigs had mansions on Grosse Ile, but nothing like this one. Sam's was three-story, with outer walls of heavy stone block, and, because of wartime restrictions on the use of steel in 1942, wood construction throughout the interior done quite elegantly. The first floor extended east beyond the two upper floors to the Detroit River, where it connected to a boathouse that housed two high-powered yachts Sam experimented with in his spare time.

In Sam's day, the first floor of his mansion had a huge living room and next to it a library filled with more books than Sam could ever have read in his lifetime. The dining room seated twenty-six at a long, hand-carved, heavy oak table. The kitchen was fit for a large hotel. A beautiful circular stairway gave access to the two upper floors with their twelve large bedrooms and attached baths, enough for the overnight guests Sam had hoped would visit but never did.

When Societe Inter Nationale bought the mansion, they professionally relandscaped the yard enclosed by Sam's high wall. Sam had preferred a lawn barren of shrubbery in the interest of security. Now the grounds of the estate had come to life. A powerful fleur-de-lis fountain that could be seen from the road was located directly across the yard from the front door. Extensive shrubbery graced the property inside the walls, and large, mature trees were installed to give balance and much-needed shade. Extensive new flower gardens added color and a touch of perfume if your smeller worked really well. I was sure Sam's obsolete security technology had been replaced by modern electronic video/computer equipment and that numerous unseen video cameras behind all these new bushes examined us in detail as we drove up.

Charles Legro himself was there at the door to greet us with a smile.

Standing next to him was Eric Gitano in a coat and tie around a high collar that covered his neck tattoo. He did not smile. His eyes avoided mine.

Charles bowed slightly, shook my hand, and said, "Welcome, my friends. Welcome to Societe Inter Nationale."

"Thank you, sir," I said. "You are most gracious to open your club especially for us. Susan and I appreciate it." It was tough saying this to someone who would have a person like Eric Gitano standing next to him.

"Susan is a good friend of the club, Paul," Legro said. "She and her family are always welcome. Come on in. Let me show you around."

An unsmiling Eric Gitano stepped aside, and we walked in.

One could see immediately that a fortune had been spent to revive Sam's mansion. The interior was open and bright now, and far larger than I remembered from my visits years ago. It took me several moments before I realized the reason for this was that the wall separating the living room from Sam's huge library had been removed, along with most of the books.

The living room, where Sam was murdered, had been gutted and, with the library gone, was now one huge party room. The floor had been retiled, and now much of it was covered with thick oriental rugs. I was not surprised to see that Legro had replaced all Sam's furniture with new, modern furniture.

Looking up, I saw that about half of the ceiling in this huge party room had been cut away. Ornate iron railings were installed at the edges of what remained of the two upper floors to allow people to lean over and observe the partying on the main floor. To top it all off, an oversized, glassed-in elevator climbed the far wall to take partygoers between floors.

So this is sky-fuck. I must say Charles Legro's dirty little mind thinks big.

Legro turned to me. "I want to apologize for the terrible mess you see here. Susan may have explained that construction people are here every day for phase two of our reconstruction project and will be for another several weeks. We're remodeling the second and third floors. To speed them up, I've allowed them to bring in the lift truck you see over there to raise supplies to those floors through the openings up there in the railings. For now, that length of rope you see up there replaces the sections of railing they removed. Of course, those missing sections of railing will be reattached before our club members return."

I looked around. The walls of this room, what Legro called his party room, were decorated in modern motif now, and from its high ceiling hung four huge crystal chandeliers. All but two of Sam Norbeck's paintings that had once decorated the walls had been replaced with new, very expensive, and very modern paintings of nudes. One needed very little imagination to guess what they were doing. Charles Legro said that well-known artists I'd never heard of had painted them.

Legro looked about. "You may have noticed when you walked in that I've relocated the portraits of Sam and Marion to a place of honor, where guests entering the mansion will see them. The placard beneath provides a brief history of Sam Norbeck's accomplishments."

Yeah, but I'm not so sure old Grandpa Sam would appreciate hanging in what his grandson Bertie refers to as a whorehouse.

Charles Legro gave me time to absorb what he'd done. Then he said, "Let's move on to the rest of the estate. Next, I'll show you the casino. Follow me."

Susan attached herself to Legro, and we passed into a casino equipped with gambling machines about as one expects to see on cruise ships.

"Paul, I'm sure you've seen these machines many times before," Legro said. "Here, the difference is that the sound of the bells one hears when winning at the machines is muted so as not to disturb the guests in the next room, which I will show you now."

We moved through a door into another room filled with baccarat tables, poker tables, and craps tables.

Legro waved his arm. "This is where the real money changes hands. Some nights the stakes get huge, even by my standards. You can't imagine. Some of my guests are addicted to gambling, and I let them play their hearts out as long as they can afford it and are not a danger to themselves or others. As long as they have the funds to play their games, I leave them alone. It's fun for them and very lucrative for us."

I had visited Monte Carlo and some of the better-known casinos in London in my past life, and although not as large, this card room rivaled them in quality, comfort, and grandeur, and perhaps outdid them in, as I had learned earlier from Bertie, intimacy. I wandered among the green tables and well-padded chairs. I could visualize the waiters with their champagne and whiskey silently moving about, the clattering of the roulette balls and the shuffle of cards, their inexorable bias gradually shifting vast sums to the internals of Charles Legro's casino.

"Charles, just how high do some of these games get?"

He smiled. "As financier J. P. Morgan was once quoted as saying, 'If you have to ask, you can't afford to play.' Millions, Paul."

Susan looked back at me, smiling, then up to Legro as if she'd never heard the comment before and was so proud of him for saying it. "Let's move on, Charles. What else have you here to dazzle Paul?"

He smiled at her. "Follow me, my dear." He led us out of the room, past the dining room to a locked double door that I recalled wasn't there years ago. He peered into a facial recognition security device on the wall, the doors opened, and Legro led us into a hallway and past a wall of floor-to-ceiling mirrors. We continued to another door, which he opened with a similar security device.

Beyond this door, I noted the faint breath of the Detroit River and the distant sound of water gently lapping against ships' hulls. We turned a corner, and there before us were his two superyachts in a huge room. They had been backed into their slips, and they were sleek, and they glistened. Two huge, vertically rising doors gave them access to the river. The doors were closed now except for an opening of about a foot above the water for one, maybe six feet for the other. I stood there amazed.

Legro broke the silence. "Paul, someday soon I hope we can get you a ride on one of these beauties. They're Sunseekers. Sixty-eight-foot Sunseeker Predators. We've overpowered them to allow them to cruise for hours at over forty knots. These beauties will give you quite a ride. We pick up customers as far away as the Lake Erie party islands and Cleveland. Occasionally Buffalo. My customers love the ride if the weather cooperates. Susan here has been on some of the trips, haven't you, Susan?"

"Yes, I have, Charles," she said, smiling up at him and squeezing his arm.

Legro let me walk around the vessels and up onto their decks and finally said, "Shall we return to the dining room for your special dinners? We don't want them to get cold."

Susan and I agreed, and we headed to the dining room in silence. As we passed through the hall of mirrors, I said, "Charles, I always heard Sam had a safe room here in his mansion. Apparently, he always feared for his life. Did you ever find it? I would love to go through it if there is one."

Looking straight ahead as he approached a facial recognition device that would return us to the dining room, he said, "If there is one, we never found it."

"Oh, I'm sorry," I said, smiling to myself. "I was hoping it would turn up."

Legro said, "I'm inclined to believe that story is all rumor. You know, there were many rumors surrounding the old gentleman. I think that may have been one of them."

It would have been rude to question him further, maybe even life-threatening if what Bertie said about him was true, so I let it drop, not even looking to Susan for an indication of her thoughts. I knew she'd heard the same story about the safe room and believed whatever Legro told her.

Legro opened the double doors again, and we entered the dining room. Off to our left was our table, beautifully set up near a large window looking out to the Detroit River and Canada in the distance.

Before sitting, I turned and said, "Charles, I can't thank you enough for what you're doing for us. I hope someday I can return the favor."

Legro bowed slightly. "The pleasure is all mine, sir. Enjoy your dinners. We are serving the specialty of the house."

CHAPTER 33

THE SPECIALTY OF THE HOUSE

When we were seated, Legro stiffly bowed again, stepped away from our table, and disappeared through the kitchen doors. Immediately, a waiter appeared carrying an ice bucket of champagne on a stand and placed it next to me. "Our best champagne, compliments of Mr. Legro." He uncorked it, waited for it to settle, poured our glasses, bowed, and backed away.

I looked at Susan and touched my glass to hers. "Here's to you, my dear."

She beamed and took a sip.

Waiters placed an appetizer before us. House-baked walnut sourdough bread with herbed goat cheese and salsa verde roasted garlic. Next came wood-grilled Spanish octopus and roasted beets with Laura Chenel goat cheese, mixed greens, and a walnut vinaigrette. For our main course, Legro selected wood-grilled North American elk tenderloin.

How could you possibly top what Charles Legro had selected for us? Well, for me, at my pay scale, the good old American chow the army served in Iraq after a week in the field could top it. But I didn't tell Susan. Or Charles Legro.

Conversation during dinner was minimal, but when I finished the last of my elk tenderloin—flavored to perfection, I might add—I asked Susan if she'd heard any more theories about her brother's passing.

"So far, I've heard nothing to suggest anything other than suicide. I don't care what the police are saying, the Reardons didn't do it. I told you why. There's no evidence of murder, anywhere. Mom refuses to believe any of her kids could kill themselves." Her eyes moistened as she slowly shook her head. "But, Paul, it is possible. We have it in our DNA. Dad did it. So why not Don?"

"Maybe because those of us who loved him can't imagine anyone as happily married as he was, and having so much fun in life."

Susan thought for a moment. "Don was under a lot of pressure. I don't think his new business was going all that well, and I heard Dickie was pressuring him to hit Mom up for a lot of money. It was the last thing he ever wanted to do."

"You heard your mom sound off at the dinner party about how they all had motives and opportunities. Doesn't that count for anything?"

"Maybe something," Susan said, "but very little. Let's face it. Motives and opportunities don't mean they actually did it. You know Mom refuses to say it, but Bertie and I had opportunity and motive too."

"Keep your voice down, Susan," I said. "And you're sure about Ellie, I suppose."

"If anyone murdered him, maybe it could have been Ellie. She was there at the garage. There's steel down her backbone most people don't see. But I know her too well to believe for a minute that she could do it. She's a sweet person. She loved him. No way could she have done it. They fought all the time—sure, we all knew it—but she could handle it. Not possible that she did it. And if she didn't do it, no one did it. Change the subject."

"Sounds like Don married a handful. Maybe they should have stayed in New York. They're a little more couth there."

Susan shook her head. "Not really. Don said they had them there too. Had to beat them off with sticks. She just has that ability when she talks to you to make you feel you're old friends from way back. She's a wonderful person, but a lot of men aren't grown-up enough to accept her the way she is. Everybody likes her. She collects friends without even trying. Mother said the other night at dinner that Ellie's planning to head back to New York when this is all over. Probably makes sense. But I would miss her." Susan seemed genuine.

By now, our waiter had cleared the dinner plates from the table, and we were savoring a generous helping of my favorite cognac, Martell Cordon Bleu XO. Next to it were the remains of what had been a steaming cup of black French coffee.

Thoroughly mellowed out now, I leaned back in my chair. "Legro has been awful kind to do all this for us. He must think very highly of you and your family."

I wondered if I was in for more loving tonight, thinking that it would certainly cap off the evening. But, of course, first things first. My snifter was empty, and one more couldn't hurt. I looked around for a waiter, and none was in sight. That gave me an idea.

"Susan, don't let anyone touch my coffee. If a waiter shows up, order me another Martell. I'll be right back."

She smiled. She looked mellowed out too.

I headed toward the men's room, but as soon as I was out of Susan's sight, I turned and headed toward the double doors that led to the boats. I'd noticed during dinner that Legro had not closed them when we returned to the dining room. I walked through and saw that one of the large wall mirrors had been moved to one side, revealing a room.

I looked around, then stepped into the room and was staggered. It was Sam Norbeck's long-lost safe room. I could see that Legro had found it and converted it to the porn studio Bertie had described, complete with beds, arm and leg restraints, a collection of whips, comfortable chairs for an audience, video cameras, and lights. Lots of lights. A door off to one side led to more rooms, two bathrooms, a kitchenette, and a dressing room with racks of costumes for both men and women. And little girls. And boys. The costumes were of all colors and shapes. Some of the dresses would fit six-year-olds, maybe younger. I imagined children preparing for show time, being given pep talks about being on TV, how to act, and how to behave in front of naked adults. They were told they would be rich. They would make their parents proud.

I turned to leave, and there in the doorway was Eric Gitano with two associates. They were short, like Gitano, and not as powerfully built. Neither would have been a problem for me if it hadn't been for the guns.

"Why the guns, guys? I'm looking for the men's room. This isn't it."

"We don't like you being here," Gitano said. "I don't think Mr. Legro will like it either when he finds out you're snooping. Stay right here, boys, while I go talk to him."

He left me in the charge of these two goons. We stared at one another. Both were wearing T-shirts and blue jeans with big leather belts and oversized metal buckles. Like bikers. Size-wise, they were no bigger than most of the Arabs I ran into in Iraq. The one on the right had to be over fifty, soft and overweight, with a well-developed pot covering the top half of his fancy belt buckle, testimony to time well spent in barrooms. The other was slim and could have used a dinner like the ones Legro had served Susan and me. When he opened his mouth, I could see he should've started brushing his teeth as a boy. I was about to make the suggestion, then thought better of it.

I edged toward them, and they backed up, moving their guns around. Guys like these would likely shoot without thinking if they got any more nervous. Probably not smart to make a move. Waiting for Gitano and Legro to return would be a better strategy. So we waited.

Their guns were heavy and slowly lowered to point somewhere closer to my kneecaps. I knew the feeling from four tours in Iraq. But apparently, they hadn't learned, as I had, not to point your weapon anywhere but at the heart of someone who wants to kill you. Right now, my gut was in full burn, and given the chance, I was ready to do exactly that. Maybe they weren't smart enough to know what was on my mind, or as probably was the case, they didn't have the on-the-job training I had.

Eric Gitano finally returned and mumbled something into the ear of Potbelly, the one who appeared a touch less dim than the other.

He flinched, looked at him, and said, "What?"

"You heard me. Do it." Gitano reached into his pocket and pulled out a pair of handcuffs. He walked behind me, slapped on one cuff and then the other, then reached into my side pocket, extracted my car keys, and stepped to my left. The cuffs were not police specials but rather had a longer chain to allow some motion between arms.

"You're going for a ride in your car, big guy," he said, looking up at me. "What do you think of that?"

"Sorry, but I'm going to need Miss Norbeck's approval before I go, and something tells me she's going to disapprove. She expects me to take her home."

"Mr. Legro is going to explain that you had to leave temporarily. He'll offer to entertain her until you return. She will accept his kind offer, as she has done many times before. She has found him to be a gracious host."

"Miss Susan Norbeck is going to know I didn't walk out on her willingly when she hears me yell out if I leave this room."

There was a motion to my left, and a sudden sharp lightning bolt slammed through my head, followed by a dead blackness. Zero, nada, nothing, as the man says.

CHAPTER 34

INDIGESTION

I began to sense movement, a lot of movement up and down, back and forth, like riding in the back of an army truck. But it was not an army truck. I was in a tiny enclosure. There was a sliver of light from two corners, and as I slowly returned to life, it dawned on me I was in the trunk of a car—a trunk very much like mine. Probably mine, because they had my car keys. My arms were still pinned behind me with Gitano's handcuffs. There was a stabbing pain in my head all this movement only aggravated, and a deep emptiness in my lungs I get when I'm out of options. Worse, I was cold, very cold, and discovered I was bare-ass naked. Nothing on, not even skivvies. Just handcuffs. Everything, including the pain in my head, was moving in every direction, and occasionally, to round out the picture, there was the faint smell of automobile exhaust. I could hear a car pass us. Then more cars. We were moving on a city street. Where?

The question was answered soon enough. The car slowed, turned, abruptly bounced up, stopped, then started forward again, slowly turning first one way and then another, stopped, and backed up a short distance. Then it stopped, and the motor turned off. Silence for several minutes. I could hear voices, a door open and close, then nothing. Finally, more voices, and at last the trunk opened, and the punk with the gut hanging out looked down at me.

He turned to his buddy and asked, "How we gonna get this asshole out of there? He's a heavy son of a bitch."

"I dunno. Wait a minute. I got an idea. Pull on his dick. He'll jump out." They both laughed. I didn't.

"You awake, mister?" one said.

"Fuck you," was all I could think of to say. But it answered their question.

"Get out. I'll help. Just don't try anything smart."

I rustled around and worked first one leg and then the other out of the trunk. Then they reached in, each grabbed an arm near the armpit, and pulled. Finally I was out of there but immediately fell to my knees, completely wiped. They waited for me to get my circulation going again, then hoisted me to my feet. I just stood there, looking around. It *was* my car, for Christ's sake.

"Stand for a minute so you can get your strength. You're going to need it."

We were in a fenced-in yard illuminated in one far corner by a weak light. In front of us was the back of a two-story brick building that looked like it had been there since World War I. Three small, chest-high windows were arranged over another row of smaller windows at ground level, obviously for a basement, several with dim light pushing through dirt that had accumulated over time. Over to one side was a door large enough to allow entry of a truck. In front of us was a short flight of steps leading to a steel door with a window with bars on it.

Bad Teeth said, "You're shivering. That means you can move. Start up those stairs straight ahead of you. Go on. One step at a time. You can do it."

I took one step and stopped. Started to tip. Potbelly returned me to vertical. I was feeling much better now, but they didn't need to know it. "That hurt, guys. Take it slow." I was thinking they had no desire to carry my 220 pounds up those stairs.

"Take your time, Mr. Steiger. We got plenty."

Finally one of them pushed me, and I took another two steps, then slowly moved to the stairs and stopped. "One of you help me lift my foot. It's not working."

"What do you mean it's not working? Lift it."

"You ever spend a day in the trunk of a car? Help me, goddamn it."

Bad Teeth put his gun in his pocket and bent down and lifted my knee. That's when I knew I had a Rhodes scholar here. Maybe there was hope after all. They pushed me up the first step, and I waited to get my balance. They were on each side of me now, holding me steady. I waited a full minute, then took a step up on my own. They followed me up. We continued up the next two steps, and Bad Teeth reached forward and opened the door. We marched in as slowly as I could make it.

Now I could hear a distant hum, like the sound of a large electric motor. Occasionally it would drop in tone as if struggling, then return to normal. We proceeded down an unlit hall to another door. Bad Teeth opened it, and we walked into a large, brightly lit room accessed to our left by the large door I had seen when they got me out of the car. All around the room were stacks of boxes and other supplies on pallets. We were on a metal walkway several feet wide and a foot or two above the concrete floor. It ended at a wide section of decking about twenty feet into the room. A railing enclosed the walkway and three sides of the wide section.

Off to one side of the room was an industrial elevator maybe thirty feet square, capable of lifting forklift trucks and supplies to and from the basement. Beyond it were stairs leading downward.

"Keep going, Mr. Steiger. You're doing fine." Bad Teeth had apparently tried out for the diplomatic corps and failed. I tripped and fell, groaned, and took my time working my way back to a standing position. I took another step and halted.

My rattled brain started to clear and figure out what this was all about. The first clue was the awful odor of dead animals. I was about to explore Bertie's dog food machine. Firsthand. From inside.

We finally got to the wide area at the end of the walkway, and Bad Teeth said, "Joe, we gotta take his cuffs off first. They don't want them going through the machine."

"Okay. But make sure you keep that gun on him. He may be faking. I'll go around behind."

I looked over the rail to see a large, round vat filled with partially digested animal parts swimming in a thick brown liquid. Two counter-rotating stainless steel blades stirred the mix, sheared the flesh, and forced it under the surface only to reappear again. A sheep's head emerged. Its dead eyes stared at me until the slowly rotating blades pushed it back under.

Potbelly put his gun in his pocket and fumbled with keys, then inserted one in the left cuff. I take it back. These were not Rhodes scholars.

The instant my left wrist was free, I swung the right arm around with the cuff still on it with all the force I had. The longer-than-normal chain between the cuffs gave it a whiplike action and allowed the opened cuff to nail Bad Teeth square on the temple. He reeled, forgot about the gun in his hand, lost his balance, and fell over the edge of the deck. And then he screamed. He held his arm out as he fell, and I watched a blade grip it and pull it from his shoulder as the next blade moved toward his head and body and pushed them into its vortex. His scream, high-pitched, almost a squeak, stopped abruptly.

Potbelly, enraged, gun still in his pocket, started toward me, thinking to push me in after his buddy. Bad idea. I was naked and slippery from sweat, and he got no grip on me.

I swung aside, grabbed his T-shirt and leather belt, and with the help of his momentum, lifted him up and over the deck railing. "He's your friend, asshole. Give him a hand."

He did. One hand at a time.

Somewhere, the electric motor strained briefly as the machine digested first one, then the other, not unusual for these motors when working hard. Bad Teeth's brief scream was not enough to alarm workers in the basement. I could hear the mutter of voices below but nothing unusual until someone yelled out, "Hey, there's a shoe coming through. What the fuck's happening up there?"

I yelled down, "Better stop the machine. There're three more shoes and a couple of oversize belt buckles in the machine. Got thrown in by mistake. Sorry, guys."

I walked out and headed to my car, wondering where I was and how the hell I was going to get this cuff off my right wrist. I looked at it and noticed, lucky me, the key was still in the lock. Problem solved. And more luck when I got to my car. The keys were still in the ignition, and my clothes, including my skivvies and socks and shoes, were in the back seat.

Still naked, I wasted no time moving the car out of there. A couple of blocks later, I stopped on a poorly lit street, only one light at the intersection up ahead, threw on my clothes, and then drove several more blocks until I came to a street sign I recognized: *Six Mile*. It was a street on the north side of Detroit. I turned right onto Six Mile and in about four blocks came to Woodward Avenue, no more than forty-five minutes from Grosse Ile. En route home, I firmly decided no one ever needed to hear how I had put two thugs into a meat grinder.

I got to the Norbeck home late. Susan's door was open. She'd heard me come in and was standing there staring at me. "Where the hell did you go? You just walked out leaving me there all alone."

My splitting headache didn't need this crap. "You weren't alone. Charles was there."

"Thank God. He's a real gentleman. Unlike you. Where'd you go?"

"Let's just say Charles had an errand he wanted me to do for him."

"What errand?"

"My dear, I'm sure Charles'll tell you if he wants you to know."

She glared at me for what seemed like a minute, then turned and went into her room and slammed the door. I was in no mood for fun and games. It would not have been fun with my broken head and her this pissed. And if she'd stepped any closer, she might have asked about the gamey smell I'd picked up running Charles's errand. Tonight I was going to enjoy nothing more than a handful of Tylenol and a long, hot shower before bed.

CHAPTER 35

BERTIE HAS SOMETHING TO SHOW ME

The next morning, I took another long, hot shower and more Tylenol and had just finished stuffing clothes into my suitcase when I got a phone call from Sergeant Chuck LaGrange. He had a lot to tell me, so I was late getting down to breakfast.

Bertie and Susan were already there when I arrived, and, of all people, Sarabella, looking far better than I'd seen her since her party. Even since our go-around yesterday afternoon. She smiled when I walked in. *Proof that reduced levels of cyanide in one's blood do wonders.*

Susan jumped up from the table, ran to me, and threw her arms around me. I'd been forgiven. Looking around to the others, she said, "Paul and I are going to be seeing much more of each other from now on."

Sarabella beamed.

I smiled briefly and unwound Susan's arms from my neck. "Greetings, all. Good to see you down here, Sarabella. You're looking great."

Before Sarabella could reply, Susan said, "I'll get you coffee and some orange juice, Paul. Sit next to me."

I had news for them. "Folks, I heard from Sergeant LaGrange this morning. The DA has officially declared Don was *not* a suicide. Don was murdered by Dick Reardon, who in turn was murdered by his wife." I glanced at Susan sitting back in her chair, slowly shaking her head. I looked at Sarabella and raised my orange juice glass to her. "You are vindicated. Don did not kill himself. The victory is yours."

174

Mattie had just started to the kitchen when she heard my news, stopped, and turned to look at me. There was a wide smile on her face.

Sarabella clapped her hands together and said, "Paul, you had a lot to do with it. My humble thanks to you, dear boy."

"As I think you all can guess, and as I declared once before," I continued, "I'm returning to Akron now. And I'm determined never to go into the detective business again. Give me the simple life of a Green Beret in wartime Iraq anytime."

Susan slumped in her chair. "So soon?"

"My bag is packed, and I'll be heading out after breakfast." I looked around. "I sincerely thank all of you for your hospitality. It's truly appreciated. I have to add that in no way was the visit boring. But let's not do it again anytime soon, okay? I'm fine with boring."

We continued with our breakfasts and small talk, and I'd just finished my second cup of coffee when Bertie looked at me, winked, briefly glanced at Susan, then got up from the table and walked over to me. He bent down and whispered in my ear, "Something happened last night you should know about. Stop by my room, and I'll show you."

I whispered to him, "I think I already know."

"Trust me. You don't."

"This won't take long, will it? I'm hoping to get going before noon."

Bertie whispered, "It may be a little long, but you won't want to miss it."

Susan was staring at us. "What did he just say to you?"

I shook my head. It was plain she was not pleased with that reply.

By the time I'd finished my coffee, Bertie had left the room, Susan was still at my side, and Sarabella was struggling to stand, holding on to the back of a chair and working to get her balance. I offered to help, but she said she was determined to make it about the house without assistance.

"Susan," I said, "I'm going to the kitchen to say goodbye to Mattie, then run up and get my bag and see what Bertie wants. I'll meet you back down here before heading to the car."

"You'll come back to Grosse Ile very soon. I know you will, Paul. It's not far."

"Far enough."

I stopped at the pantry, where Mattie was putting dishes away. "Mattie, my true love, I want to thank you for everything, including the advice you gave me."

"It was from the heart, young man. Remember that."

"And not a word of your secret will ever see the light of day. Everything's going to be all right. Love you more than you know." I put my arms around her and hugged her hard for a long time. Our eyes were damp when we parted.

From the kitchen, I went to my room to get my bag and then remembered Bertie. His door was open when I got there.

"Come in and close the door. And lock it," he said, pointing to a chair in front of his large computer screen. "It's a video of something that happened last night at the Sin Club. I apologize for the poor quality."

When I was settled, he started. The first scene showed Susan and Charles in animated discussion, probably about my sudden departure. Then they walked up the stairs and out of view of the security camera. Bertie fast-forwarded it until the shadowy outline of a man appeared entering the front door of the Sin Club. It was dark.

Bertie stopped it there and said, "Paul, that's Eric Gitano entering the club late last night. The video was recorded by the Sin Club internal security system and is a little rough in spots and sometimes not real clear. I have a hunch your imagination will fill in the blanks."

"Go ahead. I can handle it."

Bertie started it up again. Gitano walked into the party room and was startled and a little blinded when the room lights flashed on. After a second or so, he looked around to see Charles Legro secured to a chair by duct tape all around his body and extending down his legs to secure them to the back and legs of the chair. Facing him was a video camera set up on a tripod.

Legro saw Gitano and shouted, "Get out!" but not in time.

Two men emerged from the shadows, put guns on Gitano, and secured his hands behind him. One of them said to Legro, "Watch what happens to child rapists." He turned to Gitano. "Mr. Gitano, we've explained to your boss, here, that some weeks ago, you boys made a cruel mistake. You produced and distributed a video of a very young girl shrieking as she was being sexually ravished by you. You did it in front of guests sitting around on comfortable chairs, many of them enjoying their favorite drinks. Your video camera recorded it all." He waited a second for effect.

Eric Gitano remained silent.

"What you failed to realize was that the girl in question was the daughter of a close friend of someone in the audience—a person who is an associate of ours."

Legro interrupted. "Please understand … if I'd only known, I'd never have done such a thing."

"Shut up. Don't say another fucking word."

Legro began to tremble. It was barely visible in the poor quality of the video.

"Let me continue without interruption, if I may," the man said. "It seems his close friend is a gentleman with a very short temper. And when this friend, who I want to remind you is, shall we say, *connected* to a powerful family back east, was informed of what you had done to his ten-year-old daughter, he was deeply concerned. After all, it was his daughter. A ten-year-old child. And then when it was explained to him there was applause from the audience when it was over … well, I don't have to tell you how this made him feel."

The man paused, as though giving Legro and Gitano a chance to respond. Neither did, so he shrugged and continued.

"Now the gentleman understands that this is just business for you, and therefore you are unable to understand how he feels. So he asked us to visit you and impress upon you his feelings and just how upset he really is."

Now Legro tried to speak, but it came out as a croak.

"He asked me and my friend here to rectify the situation. We said we would be glad to, because, frankly, we're a little upset too. By the end of this evening, we think you'll fully appreciate the seriousness of the situation you put yourselves in." He paused again. "Any questions?"

Both Charles Legro and Eric Gitano vigorously shook their heads no.

One of the men detached the camera facing Legro from its tripod and said, "You're not going to see what happens next, Mr. Legro, but be sure to listen. I think you'll get the idea."

They led Gitano to the glassed elevator. Legro watched as the elevator ascended out of security camera range. There was a delay of perhaps fifteen minutes, while Legro vainly struggled against his duct-tape bonds.

The thugs yelled something unintelligible down to Legro, and he yelled something back to them. This back-and-forth went on for a minute or so, and then there was silence for a short period until screams were heard out of view of the Sin Club security camera. They were Gitano's screams, and they eventually changed to moans.

A descending elevator reappeared with the thugs and their camera but no Gitano. They walked to Legro and said, "We suggest you find our friend's daughter and spend whatever it takes to rehabilitate her and as many other girls as you can find that are in your porn videos. Otherwise, we're coming back to kill you. Slowly. It's as simple as that."

Legro nodded without speaking.

The two thugs walked out the front door with their camera to a car, leaving Legro bound to his chair, facing the empty tripod. The only sounds were unseen automobile doors opening and closing and then a car starting up and leaving, and occasional moans from a wounded Eric Gitano upstairs.

Bertie continued the video for a few minutes longer to show me something he felt I should see and then shut it down.

I sat back in my chair and looked up at the ceiling. The video left me physically ill. It was the third gut shock I'd had in the past three days. I was getting way too old for this shit.

Bertie copied the video to a thumb drive, handed it to me, and said, "Show this to Ellie. Then be sure to destroy it. You do not want to be caught with what's on it."

"Why in the hell would Ellie want to see that? It's revolting."

"Trust me. She'll want to see it."

"I can't believe it. No way."

"She's looking for closure."

"Why would she look for closure?"

"Trust me. She's looking for closure, just as you are. This will go a long way toward it."

"I'm heading over there anyway to say goodbye. I'll ask her if she wants to see it. But how much she wants to see is up to her."

"Just be sure to destroy it after she sees it."

I stood and shook his hand.

"Goodbye, Paul. At last we got to know each other after all these years. Hope to see more of you in the future. You're one of the good guys." He sounded sincere.

I wasn't so sure I knew Bertie at all after this but said an honest goodbye to him, left his room, and walked to my car. Ellie's home was not my immediate destination.

CHAPTER 36

INCIDENT AT THE SIN CLUB

I was surprised to see Sam Norbeck's giant wrought iron "sin" gate standing wide open when I arrived at Societe Inter Nationale. I drove through it and parked at the front door to the club, also partly open, and rushed in. I had not mentioned to Bertie that Don's external backup drive containing his Sin Club files was still in the possession of Monsieur Charles Legro. While watching Bertie's disturbing video, the awful thought had dawned on me that maybe those goons had found the drive and taken it with them. I couldn't get to the club fast enough. I prayed the hard drive was still there.

Charles Legro was still bound to the chair in the party room where his attackers had left him. His eyes were closed, and he wasn't moving. The empty tripod was still there in front of him.

I looked around. The double doors leading to the boats were still open, and the mirrors in the hall beyond the doors, one now with a diagonal crack all down it, moved off to one side, revealing the opening to what had been Sam Norbeck's safe room and was now Legro's porn studio.

I returned to Legro in his chair. He opened his eyes, looked around, focused on me, and said, "Get me out of this chair."

"I will. But I want something first. I want to know where you're keeping that hard drive Gitano got from Don Norbeck's house. I want that drive."

He squirmed in his chair against the duct tape. "Cut me loose. Gitano's upstairs. I've got to get to him. See if he's alive. Help him. If he's alive, he needs hospital care."

180

"I'm sorry, Charles, but I'm going to have to have that external drive first. Don Norbeck's portable drive. The one Ellie Norbeck gave you. Where is it? Come on. Tell me where you put it."

He just stared at me.

"Where is it, goddamn it?"

He struggled against the duct tape. I waited until finally he relaxed and said, "In my desk."

"Where's your desk?"

"My office. Third floor."

"Where in your desk?"

He struggled against the duct tape for a few seconds, looked around, then at me. "Bottom drawer, right side. But it's no good. The drive won't open. Go ahead and take it. You can have it. Then for God's sake, help Eric."

I took the stairs two at a time to the third floor. On the way to Legro's office, I saw Gitano over near the railing at the edge of the floor directly above Legro. Patrons could lean over the railing and look down from there on the partying two levels below. Gitano was lying on the floor faceup, naked, and bound hand and foot. He was covered in blood, and there was a hood over his head.

Even more bizarre was that one end of a safety rope across an opening in the railing had been removed from where it had been attached to the railing and tied around Gitano's neck, hangman style, apparently to impress on Legro that they were ready and able to hang him if he resisted agreeing to their terms. All in all, one had to say Eric Gitano had had a tough night.

Gitano was quiet for the moment, so I hurried to Legro's office. There, exactly where he had indicated, was the portable drive I was so worried he would explore. I wanted to keep going through his desk for any evidence I might find about his activities but felt I'd better check on Gitano and get him help.

I put the drive in my pocket and returned to Gitano and poked him in the chest. He jerked back to life and moaned.

I said, "Eric, I see your child-raping days are over." I had no sympathy for him. I'd seen worse in Iraq.

He didn't answer. Just squirmed around a bit.

I knelt beside him and untied his hands and moved them off to one side, then reached over and jerked the hood from his head. When his eyes adjusted to the light, he recognized me and screamed. It was guttural and loud and colorful and continued for over a minute. Finally, he yelled, "Those were your people!"

I didn't want to deny it and ruin a perfect chance to play with his brain, so I smiled and said, "Of course, Eric, and now my friends have returned. They're downstairs. We're going to take you to your dog food machine in Detroit."

I realized that I may have gone too far. He completely freaked out. Panicked and using his freed elbows and the backs of his feet, he scuttled away from me, not realizing he was inching toward the gap in the railing.

Before I could stop him—he was too slippery from the blood on him for me to get a grip—he went over the edge. I stepped to the railing and watched him fall in a perfect backward swan dive, his legs still tied together, arms outstretched, reaching for help that wasn't there. He did a perfect 180-degree turn in midair and was falling feet first and screaming when he reached the end of his rope. It was a long rope—far longer than any competent hangman would allow, and it yanked his head from his body.

The headless body landed in front of Legro. A shower of blood from severed neck arteries covered Legro's face and body. I watched him taste it on his lips. Eric Gitano's head bounced like a partially deflated volleyball and rolled to a stop in front of Legro, where it looked up at him, eyes and mouth wide open, a silent cry for help on its face.

A blood-drenched Legro screamed and screamed. I thought he'd never stop.

I ran downstairs to the kitchen and got a carving knife, then returned to the bloodied and shaken Charles Legro and cut him loose from his chair. I told him not to hire people who couldn't keep their heads in a crisis.

He didn't laugh. Not everybody appreciates my sense of humor.

CHAPTER 37

ALL ABOUT ELLIE

I was shaking now. I fumbled my iPhone open and took two tries to connect with Ellie to tell her I was coming over. Maybe it was the hint of urgency in my voice, because when I arrived, she opened her front door before I could knock.

"I heard you were leaving for home, Paul. Thanks for coming over to say goodbye. Come on in."

She put her arms around me as soon as I stepped in the door and kissed me hard. It was warm and sincere, and it felt good. My shakes were gone now. I didn't want it to stop.

Finally, she released me and backed away and thanked me for doing far more than I felt I had. She motioned me to a chair next to the sofa in the living room. "How about a coffee?"

"I think you'd better make it a martini, one for each of us. When you hear what I have to say, you're going to want one. Your morning has just begun."

She looked surprised, shrugged her shoulders, smiled, and headed to the kitchen. "Two on the rocks with olives, coming up."

She was gone for several minutes, and I looked around the room, thinking about how I was going to present to her all that I had on my mind. It wasn't going to be easy.

She returned with the martinis on a silver tray and set it down on the glass-top coffee table between us, next to a slim flower vase with one orchid. She had a broad smile on her face. Before I could say anything, she said, "You don't know this, but Don told me a lot about you while we were going together and after we were married."

I started to say something, and she held up her hands.

"Don't worry. It was all good. He was very anxious for me to meet you."

"We were good friends," I said. "I can't imagine him worrying whether I'd like you."

"Oh it wasn't that. He had a high regard for your service in the military. It was because I'd told him I knew Akron ... and that one time I'd dated a guy in Akron."

I took a sip of the martini she'd placed in front of me. Sometimes wild coincidences do happen, and I wondered if this was one. A question had been eating at the back of my brain ever since I'd first met her, and now it jumped up and tried to bite me. I took some time, trying first to decide if I should ask her the question, then, exactly how to ask it. Finally I looked at her. "By any chance was the guy's name Eddie Barlow?"

Now it was her turn to take time before answering. She sipped her martini, put it down, and looked at me for a whole minute. She didn't realize the delay had already answered my question. "He was an interesting guy."

"I guess you could say that. How did you get involved with him?"

"In my job back then, I found myself involved with all sorts of interesting guys."

"Oh, and what is it you did?"

She hesitated. "I tell very few people this."

"What?"

"I was a US Treasury agent. Sometimes I was undercover, in dangerous situations. Needless to say, you don't need to repeat that ... ever."

I smiled. "I believe you were in one such dangerous situation about three years ago."

"Oh really?"

"In Akron."

Her eyebrows came together. She hesitated for a long moment, then said, "Yes, in Akron."

"It involved emeralds, I believe."

"So you read the Akron papers. It had to do with a Mafia attack on a machine company in Akron."

"The company was the one I work for. Henderson Engineering. I'm a project engineer there."

Her eyebrows rose slightly. "I got caught up in the early stages, then got out."

"I know. I helped get you out."

"That's funny. I don't remember you being there."

"You wouldn't have. You were unconscious when we met."

"Really? Where?"

"On a bed in a hotel room. You had a knife in your chest."

"You were there in the room?"

"I was there."

"Why?"

"Eddie Barlow gave me a photo of you and sent me to your room to convince you to get out of town. I have to tell you, when I saw that photo, I was looking forward to meeting you. I got to your room, opened the door, walked in, and liked everything I saw but the knife in your chest. I thought you were dead. You looked dead."

She smiled broadly. "I'm sure they told you the knife was fake."

"Not right away."

"I was rushed out of Akron. Ever since then, I've been too busy to check back to see how that all worked out." She paused to think for a few seconds, still smiling. "I've always wondered who solved my murder."

"I'd heard you went to New York after that—something to do with boats. Big boats. Something about a yacht called *Run for Your Life*."

"That wasn't supposed to get out."

"That's all I knew, but I was curious. I wanted to find the boat."

"So did you find the boat?"

"A year or so later, I was sent to London by way of New York City. I stopped off for a weekend to visit Don before boarding a Sunday flight out of JFK for London. He'd been working there a couple of years. It was the last time I saw him. I told him about the boat and how I'd found it on the internet. We took a cab to Sinbad's, a well-known steak house on City Island, gave the driver a generous tip, and headed for the marina behind it. 'Look for a big one,' I said. 'Maybe the biggest one here.' It was not hard to spot. *Run for Your Life* was an old, hundred-foot Chris-Craft, sparkling white, in beautiful shape, moored at the far end of the dock. Getting to it was a long walk.

"Six people were relaxing and sunning themselves on the foredeck when we walked up. Four were young ladies flaked out in the sun on towels. They were wearing bikinis and looked to be starlets trying to make their way in the New York TV world, supplementing their incomes between gigs in the staterooms below deck. None looked like the gal in Barlow's photo. The other two were muscular, tattooed greaseballs in their thirties, a little one and a big one, on towels, on their backs. Each wore red Speedos and glistened with suntan oil. When we walked up to the boat, Little Greaseball, eyes closed, asked, 'Yeah?'

"I said, 'I'm looking for a good-looking gal who I heard might be staying on this boat.' I told him her name.

"'Who wants to know?' piped up Big Greaseball after raising his head, opening his eyes, and looking us over.

"'I do,' I said, getting a business card from Don and holding it out to him.

"'Take the card, Julio. He's got a card,' said the one girl with her eyes open. She seemed to be talking to the larger of the two guys, but I wasn't sure. Neither moved, so she sat up, wrestled her top up, moved over to the rail, and took the card and looked at it.

"Little Greaseball opened his eyes, looked around, finally locked on me, and said, 'So?'

"'I'm trying to find her and heard she might be here. Do any of you know her?'

"'I know her,' another of the girls said. 'She's not here.'

"'Do you know how I could find her? I ran into her in Ohio and hoped to run into her here in New York.'

"'She's not here,' said Little Greaseball.

"'Any idea when she'll be back?'

"'No idea.' So far, the only muscles he'd used were eyelids and lips. I guessed he was the one in charge.

"'Sorry to have put you to so much bother,' I said, turning to leave. 'Tell her I stopped by to say hello when you see her.'

"The girl with Don's card in her hand looked at it again and said, 'Sure.'

"I just held my hand up and waved, walking away. I looked at Don. 'Keep looking. You won't be disappointed.'"

"Apparently he did," Ellie said. "I was introduced to the owner of that boat in the course of an investigation. We were interested in what he was doing, not the doings of his crew. A friend of his introduced me to Don." She smiled briefly.

"I never thought Don would find you. You were supposed to be dead. Very dead." I finished my drink and ate the olive, and she finished hers. I looked at her and said, "I think we both need another."

She agreed. She didn't know it, but she was going to need hers more than I would need mine.

CHAPTER 38

I TELL A STORY

Ellie had two new martinis on the silver tray in her hands and a worried look on her face when she returned. She placed my martini on the glass-top coffee table between us and said, "You know, Paul, we still haven't got Don's external hard drive back from Legro. I'm scared he's going to get into it. And if he does, it's going to be a disaster for a lot of people."

I smiled.

"Not funny, Paul."

I reached into my pocket. Don's hard drive clattered on the glass tabletop.

She stared at it, brightened, and then was quizzical. "How in the hell did you get it?"

"Easy. I went over there this morning, drove through the open gate, walked in, and asked for it. Legro told me it was in his desk drawer in his office. I went up to the third floor, and sure enough, there it was."

She tipped her head slightly and said, "Bullshit."

"Not bullshit. It's a true story. A long, true story."

She smiled, reached for her drink and sipped it, put it down, then looked directly at me and said, "I have time."

I leaned forward. "Ellie, you haven't been exactly truthful with me, have you?"

She suppressed a grin.

"At the funeral on Wednesday, I could see fear in your grief. Friday when I visited you here in your home, the fear was gone."

"Time heals."

"That wasn't much time," I said. "I remember your exact words that Friday. You said there was no question Don was murdered. You said I could go home, that the problem would be handled. *Handled* was the word you used."

She was silent, and nothing showed on her face.

I continued. "Let me tell you how you knew it was murder and who did it and how it would be *handled*. The day Don died, you and Don had your fight. You told him you were going back to New York, just as you said. You purchased a New York City airline ticket at Detroit Metro. Then you changed your mind. You canceled your airline ticket and, you said, returned to your home with a policeman in tow because Don might be violent. This made me suspicious that you were buying time-stamped proof of being out of town when Don died."

"Paul, I didn't kill him."

"Let me continue. I knew Don too well to ever believe he would've hurt you. I never bought that story. I began to think you killed him *before* going to the airport and wanted a policeman to discover him and see your reaction to Don's dead body. I'm sure you could put on a good show for the cops if you had to."

"Paul, goddamn it, I didn't kill Don."

I held up my hand, palm forward. "As I got to know you, I began to have doubts."

"That's better."

"I began to ask myself if there was another explanation. What if after returning from the airport, you'd gone *directly* home? What if you went directly home and found someone waiting there for you? Someone who'd killed Don. There is no other way to explain how you were so sure you knew who killed him, unless, of course, you murdered him yourself. But I didn't want to believe that."

"Thank you for small favors."

"Let's suppose that rather than Gitano visiting you *after* the police left, as you told me, he was there when you arrived home from the airport. Let's suppose he told you to open the garage door with your remote opener. You open the garage door, and there's Don's body on the floor, car engine still running."

Ellie just looked at me.

"Gitano tells you he found Don standing at his bench beside his car with its engine running, covered in grease, complaining of stomach pain."

"Yeah," Ellie said, "I wondered about that. It was a curious thing to say."

"It explains the cyanide the autopsy found in his body."

"Cyanide? There was an autopsy?"

"They're keeping it quiet for now. I wasn't supposed to tell you."

"So?"

"Gitano tells you he wants Don's computer. Asks nicely. Said when he asked Don for it, Don's reply was rude. Really rude. I know Don. The stomach pain alone would've made him mean. Don would've been so insulting that Gitano forgot in that brief moment that Legro had not given him permission to kill Don. He would've reflexively hit Don, knocking him out, then closed the garage door so the carbon monoxide would kill him. Then he waited for you." I paused to let it all sink in. "Gitano impresses on you how serious he is to get the computer, and how immune he is from prosecution because you will be blamed for Don's death. Spouses are always the first to be suspected. You know this, and of course you're in shock from seeing Don's body on the floor of the garage. You do as he asks. You believe that only Don's manuscript is on it. What's the harm? You're confused. You're wondering why Don gave you a fake password."

"I *was* wondering, like crazy. Why a fake password? That's ridiculous."

"Now Gitano is worried. He's been there too long and doesn't want to wait to confirm if the password works. So he leaves, warning you in graphic terms what he will do if the portable drive won't open. You're scared. You'd only bought time. You are in deep shit."

"I still am. What could I do?"

"You give yourself an alibi. You know the police will suspect you of the murder if you tell them Don is dead when you go to them. So you close the garage door, tell them of your fight with Don, your plans to leave town, your canceled flight, and you're afraid to go home."

"You think they'd believe me?"

"Sure. There've been reports in the past of Don's temper and your fights, so Sergeant LaGrange believes your story, follows you home, and discovers Don's body in the garage just as you wanted. You are checking the upstairs bedrooms when he finds him."

"Then what?"

"Eventually the police leave, and now you're alone and scared of what Legro and Gitano will do when they find out the portable drive won't open. You know the police can't protect you. Not going to happen. You're desperate. This explains the fear I saw in your eyes at the funeral on Wednesday but not why the fear was gone on Friday."

Ellie smiled and waved her arms. "So on Friday I'm carefree and happy?"

"Close."

"Why?"

"I'm told you have powerful friends in New York. After the funeral, you phone them. You tell them Don was murdered and your life is in danger from the people who killed him."

"Why would they care?"

"You tell them something. Maybe that they'll lose a major investment in Don's company if Gitano kills you. You beg them to somehow *convince* Gitano and Legro to lay off."

"You think they bought that?"

"They think about it. By Friday, your friends have assured you they will *handle* the problem. This explains why the fear was gone from your eyes when I visited you on Friday and your assurance to me that the problem would be *handled*."

Ellie slowly shook her head and smiled.

"Then it gets worse for you."

"Why is that?"

"Monday, I open Don's computer, and you're horrified to learn Bertie's files are on it. Undoubtedly the reason Don didn't want you opening it without me present. You realize immediately your and Bertie's lives are over if Legro figures out how to get into that external drive. It dawns on you that a simple misspelling of my name could open Don's external drive. You may or may not have called your friends a second time to please hurry."

I had a side question at this point to be asked and answered later: did Ellie know her friends would send contract killers?

Ellie thought for a minute, then slowly leaned forward in her chair and asked, "What about Dick Reardon? Where does he fit into all this?"

"You will recall at Sarabella's dinner party, Reardon said Don had visitors that day. His exact words were, 'If it *was* murder, I can tell you who did it.' When Anne said to him it was a stupid thing to say, it convinced Legro that Reardon was not just blowing hot air. He really had seen Gitano there at the garage. That was their death sentence. The Reardons had to die."

"So who killed them?"

"Gitano visited the Reardons and killed them while we were looking at Don's computer."

CHAPTER 39

ELLIE CORRECTS THE RECORD

E llie nodded. "I agree." Then, after a long moment, she looked amused. "You've done very well. You figured out what happened."

I leaned back in my chair, smiling.

She leaned forward. "Partly."

"Oh?"

"Yes. Like you said, Gitano was here when I arrived home from the airport. I apologize for not telling you, but at that point, I didn't really know you. I didn't want you involved. I wanted you to go home. The problem was going to be resolved without your help—handled, as I said to you."

"Now I agree with you."

"But help from my New York friends is the product of your vivid imagination. Period. Full stop."

"I disagree," I said. "What you may not know is that your delegation from New York was here last night. They paid a visit to the Sin Club."

"Really? I had a delegation here last night?"

"Yes."

"Please tell me about it."

"Your friends paid a visit to Mr. Legro and *convinced* him the Norbeck family is off-limits. I'm happy to say you are now safe. I'm surprised they didn't tell you."

Ellie smiled. "That's good news. But how can I believe it?"

"Anyone who sees the video Bertie recorded last night will believe it. Bertie wants you to see it." I reached in my pocket and held Bertie's thumb drive up to show her, then carefully set it down on the coffee table next to Don's portable hard drive and my empty martini glass.

"What's this?"

"Bertie's thumb drive."

"What's on it?"

"It shows something that happened at the Sin Club last night when your friends visited. Bertie happened to be hacking their security system at the time and recorded the action. He downloaded his recording to this thumb drive. You can believe what's on it. It's not photoshopped. Bertie didn't edit it."

"Show me," Ellie said. "I can't wait."

She took one last sip from her glass, and we got up from our chairs and walked to Don's office and fired up his computer. I inserted the thumb drive and waited for it to tell its story.

"Ellie, you'd better sit down. This is going to be a little rough to take."

She sat on Don's office chair in front of the computer screen. I started the show and stood behind her. She watched the whole thing without saying a word. When the thugs departed the Sin Club, I stopped the video, removed the thumb drive from the computer, and turned to Ellie. She was speechless. She just stared at me with her mouth open.

I said, "Consider your problem ... *handled.*"

Ellie didn't reply. She sat back in her chair, coughed once, and looked away. When she could talk, she said, "Excuse me, Paul, but my friends don't handle their problems that way."

"Really?" I said. "They just did."

She slowly shook her head. "No, they didn't. Those were not my friends."

"I think they are."

"No, they aren't. That's Detroit-style justice—direct and to the point, just not very imaginative. If my friends had done it, they would've killed them and quietly removed the bodies. Legro and Gitano would have disappeared into thin air. No blood. No trace."

"If not your friends, who?"

Ellie didn't answer for maybe a minute. Then she turned to me and said, "I suggest you ask Bertie." She smiled briefly, and I couldn't tell if she was kidding or not.

"Excuse me?"

"Ask Bertie."

"Bertie? Our computer geek?"

She nodded.

"I don't think so."

Ellie nodded again and continued to look me directly in the eye. "I asked *Bertie* for help, not friends in New York."

I looked away. It took me several seconds to collect my wits.

She continued. "Bertie was glad to help. He wanted to help. He wanted to avenge his brother's murder. The child porn in that club repulses him. He invented that story about the raped child being related to a Mafia capo and told his friends in Detroit to use it. There'd been so many children abused in that club Legro apparently bought the story. If Legro had been thinking clearly, he'd have realized a member of the Mafia could never have gotten past his security people."

"Ellie, I don't believe you. You'll have to do better than that."

"Think about it. Bertie can hack that club any time he wants, but it must only be on rare occasions to keep them from discovering it."

"I know that. He told me."

"So how would Bertie know the exact time to enter their security system unless he knew exactly when the attack was going to take place?"

"Coincidence."

"You know that was no coincidence."

"Then you told him."

"No, I didn't."

"Why would you even think of going to Bertie?"

"Bertie knows a lot of people in Detroit. Don told me he has contacts in Detroit that owe him. Contacts that are entirely capable and willing to avenge his brother's killing."

"Why would any mob in Detroit risk an attack on Legro? He's a powerful guy."

"Don told me Bertie's friends in Detroit don't like all that action taking place south of their territory on Grosse Ile. They look at the gambling and porn as unnecessary competition."

I nodded. "I could buy that."

"They've been wanting to do this for a long time but until now could never get past their security. Why do you suppose those thugs were so unconcerned? Because they knew Bertie would delete any record of their attack."

"Go on."

"Bertie even opened that big front gate for them with his computer. Why do you think it was still open when you got there this morning?"

"I did wonder."

"My New York friends don't have that kind of computer know-how, particularly at a moment's notice. Bertie does."

"I'm still not buying it. That's just not Bertie."

"You're wrong, Paul. You don't know Bertie. You never did. Hell, I doubt if Sarabella knows the real Bertie."

"Maybe."

"Face it. Bertie planned the attack on Legro to avenge his brother's death."

I could only shake my head.

Then Ellie added, "Bertie told me something else."

"I know you're dying to tell me."

"After Legro has rescued and rehabilitated as many of the damaged children as he can, the clubhouse is going to burn down."

"Oh really."

"Yeah, really. It's going to be called a terrible tragedy for Grosse Ile. The place will burn to the ground. With Gitano and Legro in it. They will be found to have burned to death."

I corrected her. "Excuse me. Not Gitano."

"Why not?"

I told her about his backward swan dive earlier this morning. She gagged.

I thought to myself later as I was walking to my car, *Sam Norbeck's mansion will make a beautiful fire. Inside those stone walls, the construction is all wood. Those walls will become an elegant chimney.*

CHAPTER 40

TWO BRIDGES TO SIN

My visit had been a busy eight days, and I felt good.

Societe Inter Nationale will delay its reopening indefinitely. Don's death is avenged. The police have pronounced it was a murder by Dick Reardon, not a suicide. But we know better. Sam Norbeck's death remains a mystery. Irwin's death remains a suicide.

And Sarabella's reputation remains intact. She had visited Don after Ellie left for the airport and before Gitano arrived. She put cyanide in his Coke, but he never drank enough to kill him. He doubled over and fell to the floor, and by the time Gitano arrived, he had struggled back to his feet but was too feeble to protect himself from a blow to the head. Sarabella had not killed him. Gitano had and paid a terrible price.

My secrets will remain secrets. After all, I am a family friend.

My love life is scrambled. No change there. I'm going to forget Susan. It will not be a problem. I had stopped Bertie's video before Ellie could see Susan Norbeck emerge from Charles Legro's bedroom on the third floor after the thugs had departed the club. She'd run like a scared rabbit past the wounded Eric Gitano and down the stairs to the first floor. For an instant, she glanced over to Legro bound to his chair as she ran out the door. There was panic on her face as he begged her for help, but she kept running.

There was no need for Ellie to see that. She never will. I destroyed Bertie's thumb drive with a hammer from Don's toolbox.

My feelings toward Ellie Norbeck are strong, but I know it's way too early to think how my friendship with her will evolve. The last thing she told me before I left was to look her up when she was finally settled back in New York. I could tell she was serious. But I don't know. Serious involvement with her is impossible for a retired army grunt, now a humble mechanical engineer working in humble Akron, Ohio. Her beauty, and now her wealth, puts me completely out of her class. She will remain a close and very powerful friend to have. At a distance.

En route to Akron now, my thoughts rambled. It occurred to me that had Don selected any other title for his book, he would be alive today. I know how that title rattled Charles Legro, but I can only imagine how it had twisted Sarabella's knickers. Three of the four words in the title had done it. For Don, *Two Bridges* referred to the two bridges connecting Grosse Ile to the mainland. To Sarabella, *Two Bridges* referred to Smiley Bridges and his son, Cal Bridges, who she correctly believed knew more than they'd ever let on about Sam's murder. How much did they know? She could only guess, but somewhere in her soul, she believed they knew all the truth. Seeing their names in the title of the book had unglued her. She was sure Don had heard and intended to tell the real story of Sam Norbeck's murder.

And *SIN*, Sam's initials, was in the title because Don was telling the story of his revered grandfather, Samuel Irwin Norbeck. To Charles Legro, the title meant Don would reveal the depravity in Sam Norbeck's safe room. How often it is that tragedy blossoms in the fertile soil of misunderstandings.

Then I turned to pleasant thoughts. About Joan Worth. I phoned her as I left the Ohio Turnpike tollbooth, north of Akron, to ask if she was busy the next weekend.

She said, "See you at Moorey's."

ABOUT THE AUTHOR

Born in Detroit, Robert Vanderzee grew up in Grosse Ile, Michigan, and graduated from the University of Michigan with a bachelor's degree in mechanical engineering.

Two Bridges to Sin is Vanderzee's fifth book and second novel in the Paul Steiger murder mystery series. *The Death of Lois Janeway*, published in 2016, was the first. His work ranges from two family memoirs to a third that presents a unique concept of the universe that engages with the hotly debated question of Darwin's evolution versus intelligent design. Whether writing for the historical record, the science versus theist debate, or for pure entertainment, Vanderzee's work is meant to engage readers with new ways of thinking.

Printed in the United States
By Bookmasters